# THE ARTIST'S QUEST

# THE ARTIST'S QUEST

LaJoyce Martin

# The Artist's Quest

by LaJoyce Martin



All Scripture quotations in this book are from the King James Version of the Bible unless otherwise identified.



Printed in United States of America

Printed by

WAP

**Library of Congress Cataloging-in-Publication Data**

Martin, LaJoyce, 1937–
The artist's quest / LaJoyce Martin.
p. cm.
ISBN 1–56722–199–8
I. Title.
PS3563.A72486A89 1997
813'.54—dc21 96-53624
CIP

# Contents

## Chapter 1

# The Artist

"Are you getting tired, Grandmother Harris?" Dorrie patted the blue-veined hand, a hand that had churned a Pike's Peak of butter, sprinkled a Mississippi River of ironing, and stung the backsides of ten children.

"Toler'ble," answered the family matriarch, smoothing her cloud of white hair. "How are you coming along on the picture, Dorrie?"

"Just great, Grandmother!" Dorrie laid aside her brush and wiped her paint-smeared fingers on a scrap of unbleached flour sack. "I'll let you have a peek at it."

She moved the canvas into the line of Martha Harris's vision—to a place where the light from the mullioned window could caress it—and stepped back. "There! What do you think?"

Martha squinted through age-dimmed eyes, her thin face alert and attentive. "Why, it's plum' flattery, Dorrie! I don't look *that* good. You make me look a heap better than th' lookin' glass does. What went with all the wrinkles?"

Dorrie laughed, a sound that should have carried the carefree joys of a twenty-year-old girl but fell short. "That mirror doesn't know you like we do. I've tried to put some of the *inside* pretty on the outside of your face. Surface-wise you are beautiful, but if I could turn you wrong side out and let the world see your innerfacing, your brilliance would be blinding!"

"Aw, pshaw! Away with you! I'm just a snaggle-toothed old fossil. I can't for the life of me figger why th' whole clan wants my picture painted anyhow. It was scand'lous of them to ask you to spend all these hours a-ruinin' your weekends on a withered-up prune like me."

"I've never enjoyed a project more nor had a dearer subject." Dorrie bent to kiss Martha's cheek.

"You're a talented lassie, Dorrie. No one in our family was ever artist bent. You filled in our lackin'. There shouldn't ever be a brood without a painter. I'm glad you came along; I'm proud of you. An' I know William an' Nellie are bustin' their buttons."

A melancholy darkness spread through Dorrie without a specific cause, and some of the smile bled from her lips. "I hope they are proud of me. I've—I've tried to make them so."

"An' they're proud of Billy, too, in spite of his boyish mischief. He'll shape up into a fine man. Thirteen is still th' age of a mighty unfinished gentleman. Anyhow, I tell William that with that boy he is makin' payments on his own raisin'. William wasn't without some Billy-capers hisself. Why, I remember th' time he put a minnow in Dessie's milk. You'd'a thought he had *murdered* her—"

"He didn't tell me about that."

"Yep," Martha Harris resumed her musings. "I look

'way back an' think how empty-armed William an' Nellie would be without th' two of you. In spite of you bein' born to someone else, God matched you up perfect. Oh, I can't bear to think of a whole lifetime without tooth fairies an' corncob dolls an' bean flippers an' good-night hugs from wee earth-angels!"

"We've been blessed, Billy and I." Dorrie's words, low and pensive, held a hint of some unknown regret that did not escape Martha's keen perception.

"You've always been happy to be a part of th' Harris family, haven't you, Dorrie?"

There was a slight pause. "Yes." Then stronger, "Yes, of course, Grandmother Harris. All of you have been kind to me. I couldn't have asked for a better home."

"I'll never forget the day we found you." Martha never tired of repeating the threadbare story, and until recently, Dorrie had savored its repetition. Today she'd rather not hear it. "Alan was walkin' hisself down b'side th' river bank when he chanced upon your grandpap, Earl Taylor, rummagin' about for somethin' to feed your grandma an' th' four of you young'uns.

"Mr. Taylor was tryin' to foller th' Brazos River home when th' wagon that toted all of you busted a wheel. Billy, a newborn, was nigh death's door an' knockin' hard. Th' hapless six of you had buggied from way up on th' cap rock of Texas from a place called Seminole. Your ma had died out there an'—"

"I remember, Grandmother. I was seven. Almost eight."

Martha, caught up in the reverie, didn't slow down. "Your grandma, Eva Taylor, said that your father left when you was born—or mayhap before. Oscar an' Rufus an'

Billy are your part-brothers. Your ma saddled you with her maiden name: Taylor. Your full name was Susan Dorris Taylor. I liked th' Susan name best, but Nellie thought Dorrie fit you. It went along with Harris real fine, she allowed. Your ma's name was Mattie."

"I remember, Grandmother. I was seven. Almost eight."

Martha rambled on. "By and by, Oscar and Rufus's pa came to claim them, an' that Eli Adams surprised everyone—and prob'ly th' good Lord, too—by makin' a real good papa for them boys. But you an' Billy didn't b'long to him; you was *real* orphaned, albeit Nellie lived afeared that someone *would* show up an' claim you, not knowing who your pa was and all.

"Eva Taylor, your ma's ma, thought you were tetched in th' head an' sin-cursed because you couldn't talk. I told her that kind of thinkin' wasn't always rightsome. Miz Taylor was poorly an' scarin' th' grave herself, poor thing, an' in her bad condition she knowed she couldn't keep all of you. So Nellie convinced her into lettin' her an' William have you an' little Billy as their own.

"I never saw a happier ma than Nellie Harris made. She'd been a-prayin' for a child for ten years, an' she got a *doubled-up* blessin'." Martha's face beamed with the memory. "Why, she told me that when she first laid eyes on you—"

"I remember, Grandmother. I was seven. Almost eight."

"Miz Taylor was sure Billy wouldn't live th' night out. But thanks be to God, we was havin' th' Harris reunion, an' Chester was home for that. He had just got his doctor's license, an' he was smart on children's ailments.

His good doctorin' an' Nellie's good prayers wouldn't let Billy die.

"An' then our Chester fixed up your tongue so's you could talk, too."

"I remember, Grandmother. I was seven—"

"Almost eight, but you couldn't talk before th' operation, an' you was skittish as a wild rabbit. I remember. I was sixty-five. Almost sixty-six."

"I was a frightened child, Grandmother. The woman who kept us after our mother died cuffed me when I tried to talk and couldn't form the words. I learned that silence was my best friend."

"But all you needed was th' string of your tongue clipped, an' you was fit as a fiddle an' twice as noisy."

"I remember, Grandmother. I was—"

"Seven. Almost eight. An' now you're twenty. Almost twenty-one. An' you're th' world's best artist." Martha inclined her head toward the easel. "Just look at that!"

Dorrie wrestled with the deadlock of feeling that had taken up residence deep inside, waiting for a balance to fall on one side or the other. Some truth lifted its voice higher than Martha's.

"You're fretted 'bout something, Dorrie." Dorrie thought she had her misgivings hemmed up, but a thread of her lachrymose mood must have escaped. "A gran'ma like me that's a'ready turned to a great-gran'ma can't be tomfooleried. Is it a man?"

"No, ma'am."

"Is it the *lack* of a man?"

"No . . ."

"Then what is it, Dorrie?" Martha's probing wore no lace, sported no frills.

"I'd—I'd rather not talk about it, please, Grandmother. I might seem ungrateful. I would never want to hurt my dear parents."

"Tell it, Dorrie. It needs off your chest. Let me be th' judge of if'n it carries a hurt or no. An' if'n it does, I'll not mention it ever. It'll go clean to th' grave with me. You can trust me. Somethin' in you begs unburdenin'."

Closing her eyes for a moment, Dorrie swayed with the gale of her mental turbulence. The introspection that had started as a speck on the horizon of her mind had become a full-blown obsession. But would her grandmother understand?

"Painting your picture has intensified a desire in me to learn who I really am by birth." After the first sentence broke the dam, Dorrie's words tumbled out in a flood's tide. "Perhaps I have a grandmother who is an artist, an aunt whom I favor, or a cousin who shares my genetic background. I would like to meet them, to know them. I'd like to find my biological father. Does that make any sense to you, Grandmother Harris?"

"Prob'ly it's normal, Dorrie." It wasn't the first time Martha had hosted reality unadorned by sentiment. "Your mother married youngish, an' you could have a sprite set of grandparents a-hankerin' to meet up with you. Your curiosity isn't a thing to be ashamed of. I think William an' Nellie will be open-minded an' fair about your wonderment. They'd likely as not want you to satisfy your heart now that you're older."

The hunger that had been in Dorrie's bones leaped to her eyes. "I think I shall never feel settled until I find myself."

"I know how you must feel," Martha gave a sudden

chuckle as less weighty and newer aspects of the situation occurred to her. "You must feel just like a baby tooth a-settin' atop the gums without no root."

"And getting wiggly," Dorrie nodded. "I've dreamed that my teeth are falling out." Martha's analogy, so cryptic, had enlightened her, taking away her self-abnegation. "Now I know why."

"An' you surely don't want th' fell-out tooth under your pillow for th' rest of your life."

"No."

Martha's gaze lost focus in a perplexity that seemed to search for some unattainable answer. "But how shall you ever locate your people when you don't even know their name?"

"That's my most plaguing question. All I can do is go back to Seminole, where my mother is buried, and ask neighbors and townspeople for information. It has been several years, but—"

"You don't suppose Eli Adams could help? He was once married to your ma."

"His marriage to my mother must have been short-term, but it could do no harm to ask. Do you think he would mind?"

"I don't know why he should. Mattie's dead and gone."

Dorrie turned back to the portrait, a rewarding bit of work now almost finished. With her efforts, she had given continuity to the Harris family. This small benefaction, dropped into earth's pond, would go on reverberating to heaven's shore. Soon it would be all the relatives had left by which they could remember Martha Harris; she would be gone to her reward.

Had the thought of losing this precious grandmother

prompted the feeling of desperation in Dorrie? Why did she feel lost all at once? Her adaptability had always been her greatest boon. She prided herself in her ability to be absorbed into any group, under any circumstance. Now that same sense of belonging seemed to mock her as she lost connection with herself. How many times lately had she grasped the old Dorrie tightly, trying to hold her there, only to find her slipping away on a genealogical search? Until this veil of mystery was lifted, there could be no unalloyed happiness.

"I wish I could have painted Grandfather Harris's picture," Dorrie mentioned, trying to divert her throbbing emotions. "He must have been quite a character."

"That he was," Martha said. Her recall from bygone years sped past the iron bridge that spanned the Brazos River, going farther than the small community cemetery that lay beyond it. She was seeing the man who had stood beside her through the birth of seven sons and three daughters—and the death of one. "He was all seven of th' boys rolled up in a single pie crust. He had Joseph's big heart, Matthew's square build, William's looks, Alan's patriotism, Chester's headstrongness, Arthur's funny bone, and little Robert's love for animals. I'm thinkin' one would find it nigh impossible to sketch all that."

"It would have been a coveted challenge."

The conversation about Henry Harris did nothing to alleviate the issue that was locked in the chambers of Dorrie's brain, awaiting a key. *Who am I rolled up in one pie crust?* she pondered. *My heart will never rest until I find out.*

## CHAPTER 2

# Advice

"Miss Harris?"

When Dorrie looked up from her grade book, her gaze collided with Gabe's. A tragic struggle between hope and doubt played its drama in his eyes.

"Yes, Gabe?"

"Will I pass?"

Poor Gabe. He hadn't an artistic molecule in his brain, but he tried harder than anyone else in the class. Dorrie spent a gargantuan part of her instruction time bent over his desk, coaching him in the finer points of shading and perspective. He never grasped the concept. When finished, his smudged projects were more her work than his. But it was the last week of school, and he needed the credit to graduate.

"I am giving you a passing grade, Gabe, but please don't try to make a living as an artist." She grinned.

"Oh, no, ma'am!" A flush climbed his tanned cheeks. "I'm going to be a parson and eat fried chicken!"

"I'm sure you'll make a better parson than an artist."

"Would you like for me to drop by your class next year and bring you a drumstick?"

"I would be delighted, but," Dorrie hesitated, "I'm—I'm not sure that I will be here next year."

Gabe's eyes filled with the agony of his thoughts. "You're not getting *married,* are you, Miss Harris?" His lips wanted to say more but lacked the power.

*Ah, now she knew for sure.* Several of the young men in Dorrie's class had a crush on her, but she had just this week suspected this one. She supposed him to be near her age or perhaps older. He had missed so much school to bring in the crops that his years of education had stretched beyond the normal time frame. One had to admire his perseverance. Most would have dropped out of school long since. Men like Gabriel were hand crafted, one of a kind. He had started with rare raw material and continued despite all of life's attempts to kick him in the shins. Any number of stumbling stones could have turned Gabe into a quitter, but he avoided them all.

"No, Gabe, I'm not getting married."

He laughed, a little desperately. "Not that it would be any of my business, Miss Harris. But—I'm glad."

The dismissal bell bonged, precipitating a noisy exit of pupils. The closer the summer break, the rowdier they became. She would miss them next year. . . .

Times were changing. The modern, red brick building was a far cry from the one her adoptive father had attended in Brazos Point. He told stories of slates, split-log seats, and a colicky pot-bellied stove. Now there were high, clear windows, a water tank with a spigot in every classroom, desks with inkwells and pen troughs, and a special parking section for horseless carriages out front. Education had come a long way.

The shuffling of feet died away, but Gabe stood rooted. Dorrie closed her grade book, comfortably aware of his closeness, of his clean, earthy smell. The silence welled around them, and Dorrie tried to think what to say or to do next.

"I'm taking a trip, and I'm not sure that I will be back by September," she explained.

"That's nice." His smile was as artificial as if it had been carved on a pumpkin by a knife. "I wish you a lovely vacation."

"It isn't exactly a vacation—" Dorrie's need to talk about her search—to someone, to anyone—overpowered her. "It is a business trip of sorts."

"You are looking for another job, aren't you, Miss Harris? Trying to teach me to draw gave you teacher burnout." A shaft of light from the west window was caught in Gabe's dark, close-cropped hair that coiled like watch springs.

"Actually, I am launching a search for my missing family, and I have no idea how long it may take to locate them. I was adopted by the Harrises when I was seven years old. My mother is dead, but I know nothing of my father. I want to find him."

"Haven't you been satisfied with the family who reared you?"

"Yes, very. But somewhere deep within each of us is a yearning to find our cornerstone, don't you think?"

Gabe sobered as though her question had thrust some sacred obligation upon him. "Perhaps so," he said, "but may I offer some advice?"

Dorrie liked his frankness, the absence of guile. "Certainly, Gabriel." His name, spoken without abbreviation, danced hauntingly and thrillingly in her mind.

"I've no right." His face was filled with genuine concern for her.

Why had she failed to notice his rugged handsomeness as he sat in her classroom day after day? "I would welcome your counsel."

"I just wanted to say that you must not go with preconceived ideas, Miss Harris. When you find your family, they may be different from what you expect. Our imaginations can paint misleading pictures. They may not have the same value system as your own. It's possible that they will not even be Christians. Above all, give yourself adjusting room. Take things a little at a time—but there, I've said too much."

"Not at all, Gabriel." One who had not been through like experiences could not impart such wisdom. Curiosity nibbled at Dorrie. What had this young man endured? Where did he find this insight? He might be lacking in the realm of art, but his discernment was profound.

"Was your life always predictable, Gabriel? Tell me about yourself."

"I don't like to talk about me, Miss Harris, but if it will help you—"

"I think it might help."

"I know all about changes. I've been pitched about most of my life. When I was eight years old, my father died of snake bite. My mother, too ill to care for me, placed me with a family in Dallas whom I had never met. I was accustomed to the farm, to feet free of shoes, a swimming hole, and sleeping on a pallet. City life was different: a life of pinching boots, fried shirts, and brick streets. I felt like a caged bird. The adjustments I was called upon to make were difficult, but I survived.

"Three years later, when I was eleven, my mother recovered enough to remarry. She took me back; another drastic turn awaited me.

"My stepfather was an unreasonable man who worked me like a slave and cursed at my immature mistakes. He left three years later—when I was fourteen—and I became the man of the house. That wasn't easy either.

"Today my mother lies at home quite ill. I hope that she will live to see me graduate; it is for her that I have forged on against all opposition. Then when she is gone, I will have to refocus again."

"I've lived a sheltered life with few changes," admitted Dorrie.

"I hope that you are not disappointed in your search, but bear in mind that some of life's greatest blessings come out of temporary defeat. And one other thing: You must be careful about making comparisons, Miss Harris. When you find the people that you seek, they may be less prosperous—or more so—than your present family. Comparisons would be unfair to either group."

Perception. In terms of art, Gabe possessed none. Yet in everyday life, in the things that mattered, he was well endowed. He had just bestowed upon her a gift, the materials for a future she must build for herself. No one else could have done it so selflessly, so openly.

This young man had sat in her class day after day, wrestling with a brush in his oversized hands. Now she truly saw him for the first time; a light shone from his heart, and Dorrie could see the layers of his being all revealed. She saw him, and she loved him.

"Oh, thank you, Gabriel! I needed that advice. It's a crazy venture, no doubt. But I cannot feel whole until I find out who I really am."

"I think you lack nothing, Miss Harris." Gabe's ears took on a flaming tinge. "I mean, after all, it's not where one comes from that matters so much as what one makes of himself when he becomes a new creature in Christ."

"Well said. And yet I find that something within me cannot settle into my tomorrows until I do battle with my yesterdays," insisted Dorrie. "What if my father or my grandparents need me? If they know not my Savior, then I am obligated to introduce them to Him. I may not find a single clue to lead me to my lost family, but for my own tranquillity I must make the effort."

*Please don't go, Dorrie.* Gabe didn't say it, but it was the pleading cry of his soul. Instead he said, "God go with you, Miss Harris. You will be in my daily prayers."

Then he took both of her hands, generating in Dorrie a nameless emotion of unutterable mystery and sweetness. It swelled until it reached her throat. For one brief instant, there seemed no need to rush or plan, to wish or regret. A completeness washed over her.

"I would like to go with you and hold your hands all the way to your destination, Miss Harris. I would like to protect you from any disillusionment or thwarted expectations that might arise. I would like to share your joys if joy awaits you at journey's end. I realize this is impossible. However, where I cannot go, God can, and I will ask Him to take my place. Please remember that He will never leave you nor forsake you."

The moment of closeness receded when a student

returned to the classroom for a forgotten item. As he moved into the hall, Gabriel's tall figure blurred from sight, growing dim through Dorrie's tears. Then he vanished.

## CHAPTER 3

# Revelation

On Saturday morning, Dorrie made her way to the home of Eli Adams. Grandmother Harris had said he might sprinkle some light on Dorrie's family tree. He'd been a branch grafted in for a short and blighted season.

The morning was warm; the arpeggio of crickets announced their approval of a pleasant day. A dozen shades of green grass carpeted the knolls and flats, thick and lush, paying homage to spring's abundant rainfall. Although the bluebonnets had already seeded out, the larkspur bloomed in profusion. To Dorrie, Bosque County was the loveliest spot in the world.

In a spate of childhood memory, Dorrie envisioned West Texas as a bleached and barren country with not a leaf of greenery. It was a lonely and hard land where flowers and fruit were not. She recalled straight and dusty roads, a violent sun that shone boldly, and wind that blew hard as if to take the sand back to the desert where it had once been. The temperature seesawed from deadly heat in the summer to freezing cold in the winter.

But wait! Gabriel had warned her not to make comparisons. He said that wasn't fair. And that went for topography as well as humanity. Brazos Point was blessed with the advantage of more moisture. . . .

Eli and Molly Adams lived in the old home place that had been a haven for Molly's grandmother, the unforgettable Granny Myrt. Myrt was a legend in the community, having played the pump organ at the church for sixty-seven years without missing enough services to count on one's fingers. The house had been remodeled and modernized to accommodate the five Adamses.

Oscar and Rufus, Eli's sons and Dorrie's half-brothers, were very near adulthood themselves. They were eighteen and nineteen, respectively. Then Eli and Molly had one child of their own, a boy named Jacob. He was ten.

Molly welcomed Dorrie with elaborate enthusiasm. That was Molly's way. She loved visitors anytime from anywhere, announced or otherwise. No appointment was necessary to kindle her hospitality.

"Why, come on in, Dorrie!" she burbled. "You're just in time for a fresh blackberry muffin. And how are the Harrises? Are you glad that school is out? What will you *do* with yourself this long summer? If you get bored, I'll send Jacob over to keep you company, and you won't have a dull moment."

"We're fine," Dorrie answered, trying to take the questions in chronological order. "And yes, I'm glad that school is out, and I do have plans for the summer."

"How is dear Martha? You have been visiting with her this morning?"

"Not today. I've spent several weekends painting her portrait. She will be glad to have a rest from me."

"I must see the portrait."

"It did turn out well."

"As all your work does. How I wish that I had a picture of Granny Myrt!" Molly was a chatty sort, and no subject lagged with her. "Wouldn't I have cherished a ferrotype of her sitting on that three-legged organ stool? And to think that my Jacob didn't even get to see her. He's going to be musical, too. Why, he fixed some strings on a tin washtub and can actually play a tune on the thing!" She giggled.

To accomplish her purpose, Dorrie realized she must take the conversational reins and steer them in the proper direction. "Is Eli here?" she inquired.

"He's feeding the chickens. He'll be right in."

"I came to ask him a few history questions."

"He never was good in school, Dorrie. I think he said he flunked history."

"The questions are about my own background. I am planning a trip to visit my mother's grave. I had hoped that Eli might be able to tell me the whereabouts of my father's family. I—I don't even know my father's name."

"He has never mentioned your father."

"You don't think he'll mind my asking, do you?"

"Oh, no! Eli will do anything to help a body. Is there some special reason you need to reach them, Dorrie? I've read about people needing medical information—"

"It's just a quest of the heart."

"I see." Molly touched Dorrie's hand. "Both of my parents died before I had a chance to know them. I felt cheated. I loved Granny Myrt, of course, and I can't imagine what I would have done without her. She was my mother's mother, but—" She stopped abruptly. "I hear Eli coming now. Would you rather talk with him privately?"

"No. I have nothing to discuss that the ears of the world wouldn't be welcome to hear. Please stay."

Eli came in with tufts of straw clinging to his boots, tattling of his time spent in the barnyard. "Welcome, Dorrie. Did you come to see those incorrigible brothers of yours?"

Dorrie noticed that the years and a sprinkling of gray hair had done nothing to detract from Eli's good looks. It was easy to see why her mother, or any woman for that matter, could have overlooked serious character flaws to fall in love with this man.

"Really, Mr. Adams, I have come to ask you a few questions before I go out into the world to seek my fortune."

"Beware of the big bad wolf," he countered. "He might be dressed up in your grandmother's bonnet."

"I'm on a quest to find my natural father."

"Curiosity?"

"It's more than that. Some voice, some spirit from a distance calls me. I want to know who I am before I marry and have children of my own."

"I don't see that it would matter—"

"To a woman it does matter, Eli," intercepted Molly. "I know how Dorrie feels. The unknown bothers us females, and—"

"Do you happen to know my father's name?" Dorrie interrupted before her courage failed.

"Yes," he said, "I do. You bear his name."

"Taylor?"

"His name was Charles Dorris. You were Susan Dorris until your mother's marriage to your father came to an end. Then she added Taylor so that your last name and hers would be the same."

"I see. What happened to my father?"

"That I do not know. Mattie never knew. Their marriage—if it could be called that—only lasted a few days. Mattie was fifteen. Charles left her in Seminole and never returned. After a year of his unexplained absence, Mattie had the marriage annulled.

"I met your mother when I worked for the telephone company. Our union—hers and mine—was a rebound for both of us. Except for the boys, I would mark it off as a sad mistake. Rufus and Oscar were born less than a year apart, and I failed to take my responsibility as a father. By the time Mattie was seventeen, she had three babies. How the poor dear managed, I don't know. Her survival was no thanks to me." Eli dropped his eyes, ashamed.

"I led a wayward life for several years, running from myself and from God. When I returned to make amends, I learned that Mattie had gone to a better place. The neighbors told me that she got religion before she died and that she went peacefully." Eli's story snagged on thorns of regret. "Today I am a sadder, a wiser and, I hope, a better man."

"Charles Dorris," repeated Dorrie. "At least I have a name to begin my search. Have you any idea where he was from? Did my mother meet him in Seminole? Was he a local man?"

"I'm sorry, I have no information to give you. I suppose he went to Seminole to work in the oil field; that's what took most people there. Mattie knew almost nothing about him, and I knew less. She was bitter. Nothing justifies bitterness, but she had a right to painful memories.

To bring up his name caused a fight."

"He does not sound like a father I could be proud of."

"Time and circumstances can change a man, Dorrie." Absolute certainty breathed in Eli's voice. "God gave me a second chance. If you feel in your heart that you should look the man up, I'd say do your duty as you see it."

"I shall, Mr. Adams."

"How long do you plan to be gone, Dorrie?" questioned Molly.

"That depends on how things go," Dorrie answered. "I've been with Mom and Dad Harris for fourteen years. Equality demands that I give some of my life to my own people, wouldn't you think? I may have a grandmother who yearns to meet me. If *I* were a grandmother who had a granddaughter I didn't know, I would want time to become acquainted with her," Dorrie reasoned. "And I may have scads of cousins to meet."

"How do William and Nellie feel about your quest?" Eli wanted to know.

"They're—they're trying to understand how I feel. And I'm trying to understand how they feel. It has been especially hard for Mother, and Billy is pitching a fit. But they will come to grips with it. They love me enough to want me to be happy. And I love them the more for it." Dorrie arose to leave.

"I hope that your investigation ends lovely, Dorrie!" Molly gave her a hug. "And I believe that it will."

## Chapter 4

# Leaving

Since the afternoon rendezvous when Gabriel had fortified her with his sagacity, Dorrie had not seen him again. He didn't attend the last week of school. He'd sent a note saying that his mother was seriously ill and would Dorrie be so kind as to turn his grades in to the superintendent. He had signed off with "Deepest devotion." Dorrie wasn't sure what that meant.

Gabe's absence from the classroom created a vacuum as though a candle had been blown out or the sun had been lost behind a cloud, but Dorrie didn't take time to evaluate the vague hollowness she felt. Preparations for her upcoming trip absorbed her, holding her in a surreptitious spell.

Her portmanteau was packed to bulging capacity and sitting beside her bedroom door. Tomorrow she was leaving. She felt calm, though slightly cold, and as strong in her decision as she had been when she made it. The direction she had given her will blunted any branching of thought.

Her last night at home seemed but a few starlit

moments, an hour of gray fog and then the lighting of dawn. The big day had arrived.

Breakfast was a dismal affair with Billy dabbing at his swollen eyes. He had slept little. "Do you *hafta* go, Dorrie?" he implored.

"Yes, Billy." She fought a fester of irritation. The question had become monotonous.

"But *why*? Don't you love *us*? Haven't I been a good brother?" All the pent-up passion of a thirteen-year-old rode in his words.

Poor Billy! He would never understand the restlessness in a woman's heart as old as eternity: the desire for knowledge denied her. The genes had been handed down from Eve in the Garden of Eden.

"Yes, I love you, Billy. You have been a wonderful brother."

"If you'd just tell us when you're coming back, we'd be gladder," he sniffed.

"I'm sorry, but I have no idea what the future holds for me, Billy. I don't know how long it will take to find my relatives. But I will write to you."

"You will?"

"It's a promise. I am taking stationery and stamps."

"And you'll write to me, too, and draw me a picture of a tarantula?" teased William, trying to lighten the mood.

"To you, too, Daddy, but twice as often to Mother, and her letters will be thrice as long and have sketches of Gila monsters." The vow coaxed a tight smile from Nellie, but her mouth was thin with pain.

"You are sure that you have sufficient funds, Dorrie?" prodded William. "I don't want you running short of money to get home on."

"I have plenty, Daddy. I have saved most of my wages from the past two years of teaching. I will spend wisely and carefully. If I need more, I can always paint a few portraits. I am taking my art supplies. Rich people pay enormous sums to see themselves on cloth. Please don't fret over me. I'm—twenty."

Silence fell over the table again, a thick and choking stillness. Turning her eyes out the window, Dorrie tried to ignore it, grateful that the gloom didn't reach beyond the perimeter of the breakfast room. The morning was clear and bright, spraying the earth with a golden sheen. She couldn't have chosen a nicer day to begin her quest, and she was anxious to be on her way.

The next hour crawled by like a snail, and then it happened all at once. She found herself rushing through the long, high sitting room. The familiar surroundings—the polished bookcase, the chair with its flowered slipcover, the round lamp table with its blue spread—commanded hardly a glance. However, once outside, Dorrie paused to look back toward the home of her youth, trying to memorize its features.

It was a splendid structure, friendly and unpretentious, made of native stone and heavy timber. The detailed workmanship gave credit to the mind of the man who built it against time and pillage. English ivy smothered the east wall. She would be back someday. *Or would she?*

Her mind was cluttered and clogged with whirling thoughts, and then the four Harrises departed for the railway station. Upon their arrival, a panorama of activities played out its energy. Billy was trying to talk, and Nellie was shushing him. William was transferring her grip to the porter, a squat, squarely built man with a craggy face and swelling muscles. A thousand unknown scents and sounds surrounded Dorrie, and suddenly she wanted to clasp her family to herself and take them with her.

*Our first instinct is to cling to the familiar.* She'd read that somewhere. Stretching could be painful, the article explained, but if our lives were to reach out to help and touch others, stretch we must.

"Well, daughter, it's time to say farewell," William said, laying a hand on her shoulder. "Take care of yourself." A man who hid his emotions, he delved for more words to say and found none.

Billy pulled the bill of his cap low to hide his eyes while Nellie stanched her tears, waiting to cry in private. Dorrie rushed away, not trusting her response. She didn't look back.

Reeling in the tardy part of her essence until she had collected herself, she fell into the first available seat on the train, welcoming the spitting and jerking of the engine as it complained its way out of the depot, dragging its load of passenger cars along. Her ticket would take her to Lubbock, and from there she would catch a coach to Seminole. Now that she had made the break, a keen, fierce vigor flooded her mind and body; the strong presence of spirit with which she had tackled many of her classroom problems came to bolster her. It was a good feeling: independence. The future shimmered with adventure.

While taking stock of her surroundings, a habit of hers wherever she went, Dorrie noted a thin, pale-faced woman across the narrow aisle. Her iron gray hair, scraped back from her forehead and rolled into a knot, seemed to be trying to flee from her mud-colored eyes.

Dorrie smiled at her but received no reciprocating warmth. Presently, the woman got up and moved, and Dorrie was quite alone.

The porter said it would be a trip of two and one half days. With fresh purpose and new sights, Dorrie's patience bore the initial hours well. The landscape rolled by in leagues of slow ascent or descent crowned with mounds of timber-topped hills. Occasionally, the train halted briefly at stations. Dusty little communities jogged by with their huddle of buildings, some of them patched until they could stand no more patching. Finally, the last bit of blue sky yielded to the oncoming of dusk. Her first day of travel was behind her.

She made her way to the women's sleeping car, where the tiny cubicles sadly lacked the comforts of her own feather mattress at home. *Gabe said not to make comparisons. . . .* That warning encompassed not only mortals and geographical advantages, but personal luxuries as well.

The lady Dorrie had observed earlier took the bunk below her. Except for her snoring, the woman made no sound at all. At least, Dorrie conceded, she could be glad the fellow wayfarer wasn't a whiner or a grouch or a gossip. Sometimes silence was golden.

Dorrie raised both the window and its shade, allowing the cooler night air to blow in. It fanned her heated body. She tried closing her eyes, but the longer she lay the more animated she became. Excitement robbed her of sleep. When night's early blackness had passed, the glimmer of a morning star brought the peace and beauty of a rare painting. Faith welled up in her heart, whispering that all would soon be right in her world. Tomorrow would be better than the best she knew today.

Toward morning, she slept. And she dreamed. In the dream, she was swimming toward a remote shore, but the shelf of land never got any closer. The water deepened with every stroke until it closed over her head. Gasping, she awoke in a sweat of panic, consumed by fear. She lay awake until the dim outline of canyons gleamed crimson and the deep cliffs outside her window belched forth a blue mist. Then she fell asleep again.

The next day of her journey dragged by, more tiring. The vista had changed, swathing the entire countryside in grays and browns and golds, indicative of the high plains. An outlying haze hung drab and smoky. Here and there, a splotch of dry wheat lay back from the wind; at a distance it seemed to shimmer and retreat in its attempt to escape the merciless sun. Lava from spent volcanoes claimed some of the landscape.

What was that smell? Ah, yes. Sage. The wind wafted the sweet aroma to her nostrils, bringing back poignant childhood recollections. Her mother had loved the smell of sage.

Perhaps, she reasoned, had she not been at such an impressionable age—seven, almost eight—when she was transplanted, the yearning to search for her beginnings would not be so compelling. If she had no memory of her mother—the odors she liked, the colors, the sounds—there would be no call on her heart. If nothing had preceded her life with the Harris family . . . but something had.

At noon on the third day, the locomotive crawled into the Lubbock terminal, bypassing warehouses with crude platform entrances where tired horses stood waiting. It wasn't a pretty place, and she was glad this wasn't her final destination. Clutching her handbag, she tried to stand too soon and was slammed back into her seat by the sudden braking of the train. "Just a minute, ma'am," cautioned the conductor. "Please remain seated until the car comes to a complete stop. We don't want any injuries, especially to a beautiful young lady like yourself."

The first leg of Dorrie's pilgrimage had ended.

## Chapter 5

# Information

Seminole was a bleak, windswept town that squatted on a barren locus of wilderness. The skies were clear and the air light, commodities that cities with two thousand feet less altitude could not boast.

Some thirty families lived in adobe shacks all cut from the same pattern. The success of these inhabitants could be read in their dwellings. None of the settlers were prosperous; many were poor. Poverty and idleness brought their attendant quarrels and wretchedness.

There were no hotels, but when Dorrie inquired about lodging at the rundown cafe on Main Street she was directed to a house with a lean-to room for rent. It was not an arrangement she would have espoused, but she was a victim of necessity. She hoped that she didn't have to depend on this cook with dirty hands for her food.

By the time she hired her portmanteau delivered, negotiated for her shabby quarters, and killed two wicked-looking spiders, her body was one giant strife of stinging nerves and bursting head. *Changes. Adaptability. Gabe said—* She chopped the thought in half; she didn't want to think of Gabriel today.

Determined not to spend a moment more than she must in this deplorable place, she began her inquiry at once by engaging her landlady, Mrs. Hogue, in conversation.

"I was born right here in Seminole," she mentioned. "I have returned to find my family. I don't suppose you would remember my mother, Mattie Taylor?"

"Mattie Taylor," repeated Mrs. Hogue. "That name doesn't bring up a face. How long ago has that been?"

"Fourteen years."

"Oh, I've only been here five, and that's five too long. We came from Louisiana for the oil and lost our shirt. I hate this place."

"My mother was buried here. I've come in search of my father, Charles Dorris. I have hopes that some of the old-timers will remember him."

"The oldest person here is Mariposa Carrow. Gossip has it that she was once the sheriff. I wouldn't know. She has been sickly, and some claim she left town. People come and go like Solomon's chariots in these parts. They come, gamble away everything they have, and go away bare to the bone."

"Where does Mrs. Carrow live?"

"*Miss* Carrow," corrected the informant. "She never married, and to call her a matron would be the greatest of insults. She lives a block past Parker's General Store and to the left a block in a house with two front doors—the only house in town with two front entrances. You can't miss it."

"Thank you, Mrs. Hogue. I shall try to locate her."

Dorrie remembered the general store, except when she lived in Seminole it wasn't Parker's. Her mother had sent her to the merchant often for a loaf of bread. It was an unpleasant recall. She could still hear the old man who clerked at the store barking at her. "Tell that ma of yours that this is the last piece of bread she'll get from me on credit! Tell her Old Man Marson said to pay up or shut up!" His thundering frightened Dorrie.

She was sure that she could find her way to her birthplace from the store, and a craving to see the dwelling engulfed her. Following her impulse, she walked south until she found the piteous building situated at the end of a row of tumble-down hovels. It was the meanest of them. A gnarled mesquite tree leaned against one sagging wall as if to prop it up, salvaging it from complete collapse.

There had once been a small garden such as the hand of a weak woman had time and strength to nurture; water for it had to be hauled by hand. A stalk of volunteer okra stood dried and woody. Dorrie remembered her mother making numerous trips to a windmill just outside the city to cultivate her paltry plants.

Pulling back the sagging door, Dorrie made her way into the ruins of the house that anticipated just a strong breath of wind to send it toppling. There was only one room, dark and almost bare. Only a metal bed frame remained. With closed eyes, Dorrie imagined her mother lying on that bed. *Oh, mother,* she whispered, *what a life of deprivation you lived!* A good cry would have made her feel better, but tears, with their purging, had never seemed farther away. The high-pressure voltage somewhere in her interior short-circuited them.

From the old home place, Dorrie went to the cemetery. It was important that she reconcile herself with the memory of her mother before tackling the task of tracing her father. However, she found no marker for Mattie Taylor, and many graves had been added over the years, changing the periphery of the burial grounds. She would never know the exact resting place of her birth mother.

Her head still throbbed with a wretched pounding, but she forged on. *One more call today,* she told herself, *and then I will rest.*

Along the hard-packed street that showed years of travel, she plodded to Miss Carrow's, praying that her visit would prove successful. A few heads protruded from doors and around corners. A lizard shot like a rusty streak across the sand in front of her, leaving a slender trail behind him. The day had been full of strange people and new experiences.

Both doors stood open wide at the house of two front doors. Dorrie knocked, and the voice that greeted her held no welcome. "Go away," the articulation demanded.

Dorrie would not accept defeat. She stepped inside and almost instinctively took a step backward. The unsmiling, expressionless face was the same one that had made the rail trip with her, only the woman looked even frailer now.

Miss Carrow sat in a cane-bottomed chair, the bluish shadows under her large eyes giving her the appearance of a newly hatched bird. Those eyes challenged Dorrie with the gaze of a woman who had left events behind her.

The cottage was as clean as a bleached skull and as cheerless. "Miss Carrow?"

"Go away." The voice was scarcely audible.

"Are you ill?"

"Soon be dead." She blinked against the light that glinted in her muddy eyes.

"I'm—I'm sorry. I saw you on the train."

"I went to Houston to a doctor, but he said he couldn't help me." The tone was acidic; the owlish eyes gleamed fiercely.

"Is there anything I can do for you?"

"Water. I'm too weak to lift the water barrel."

"Where shall I find water?"

"A cistern. Behind the house."

For the next two hours, Dorrie worked diligently to try to bring comfort to a woman who was losing her grip on life. She made several trips to the well, then heated water on the stove and bathed Miss Carrow. She cooked a broth from the withered roots she found in the ancient cupboard. The meager soup offered a poor excuse for food, but it was food nonetheless. In her cauldron of furious activity, Dorrie almost forgot her mission.

When the elderly woman's body was warm from the soup and she seemed more comfortable, Dorrie pulled up a chair minus so many strands of cane that it scarcely supported her. "Miss Carrow," she began, "do you remember a Mattie Taylor who used to live in this town?"

"I couldn't forget her," croaked the old lady. "She was an untamed thing for a piece, but then she got religion and never a purer soul went to meet whoever collects passports at the end. Nobody could believe the change in Mattie, leastwise myself. I hadn't any brook for religion until I saw what it did for Mattie Fay. One day she was a sinner, the next day a saint, just like that. And then she died and left four youngsters. . . . Whatever halo she got, she paid for. I always wondered whatever became of those children."

"I am one of them," Dorrie said. "The oldest."

"You—?" Miss Carrow gaped at her openmouthed. "You are little *Susan*?"

"Yes, I am. I was reared by a family in central Texas by the name of Harris. They gave me a good education and a lot of love. I'm a teacher."

"Well, if that wouldn't make the devil gnash his teeth," exclaimed Miss Carrow irreverently. Her resistance disintegrated. "You are Susan, eh? What brings you back to this forsaken perdition?"

"I'm trying to track my natural family."

"Didn't you remember that your ma died? You were old enough to—"

"I do, but I am looking for clues to the whereabouts of my father, Charles Dorris, and his family. Do you remember him, too?"

"How could I forget him? I was the sheriff. I lost count of the times I booked him."

"For what?"

"You name it; he did it. Drunkenness. Brawls. Theft. Here in this blundering place, evil men do good things, and good men do evil."

"He must have been a bad man."

"No. He was young and irresponsible, Susan. He never grew up."

"Do you know where he is now?"

"I could guess, but I wouldn't want to say. It's hotter there than it is here."

"Farther west?"

"No. Underground. I heard that he got himself killed."

Despair held Dorrie in its cruel clutches. "I had hoped to find him."

"I'm sorry, lass. Hope has a way of lifting you to the sky and then casting you down."

"Had he living parents? Brothers or sisters? Do any of them live here?"

"He wasn't a native of Seminole. I don't remember where he hailed from; he came here for work on the derricks like all the rest." She turned her eyes, the only lively part of her, to a dust-covered chest that sat in the corner. "The records would likely tell."

"The records?"

"All the criminal histories are in that wooden box. I am determined that Sheriff Dodd won't get his hands on them. If he does, it'll be over my dead body. Can you pull the files over here closer?"

Dorrie moved the heavy drawer to the center of the room, scaring a rat that retaliated by scaring her. "You look under the D's, Susan, and see if you can find Charles Dorris. My eyes aren't fit for anything."

With fingers that fumbled with a fusion of dread and satisfaction, Dorrie sifted through the yellowed pages until she found her father's record. "Here it is!" she exclaimed.

"Hand it to me," commanded the crone. She focused the page to within inches of her nose. "Yes, the information you need is recorded right here. Charles Dorris was from Briscoe County—that's Texas—a place called Tule Canyon near Silverton. His mother and father are listed as residing there. Their names are Slocum and Iantha Dorris. Chances are good that one or the other of them is still living."

"Do you know where Briscoe County might be?"

"It's about a hundred and fifty miles north and east of here as the crow flies. Catch the wagon going to Amarillo, and drop off in the canyon's mouth right near its front teeth. It should be about time for their summer trip." The dying woman was tiring; her breath came in whistling pants.

"You are overexerting yourself, Miss Carrow. Please let me help you to bed before I leave."

"No, lass. It's kind of you to offer, but I'm not ready to lie down yet. If I go to bed this early, the night will be an eternity long."

"Is there anything else that I may do for you?"

"Please take the iron lids off the cook stove so that I can have a little heat tonight."

"It's very hot in here—"

"When the sun goes down, the night air bites at my old bones."

"Shall I find you an extra wrap?"

"No, I'll be fine."

"Then I shall go and let you rest. But I shall be back to visit you again tomorrow. Good night, Miss Carrow."

To the west, the sunset burned pure gold, too brilliant for Dorrie's eyes. Was this a portent of her future? For a span of time, her mind ran on ahead, impatient to seek, to find, to know. Would they be there, those lost grandparents who would supply the missing link in her chain of ancestry? After twenty years, would they be alive and at the same address? Hope kept her spirits up, the hope that here, today, she had found a key and with it the power to unlock her past of mystery and promise. That key would bring her quest to an end.

## Chapter 6

# The Long Week

The plain faded into hazy obscurity as Dorrie pondered her way back to her room. She had eaten little all day, and now she fell prey to the gnawing pangs of hunger. Surely Mrs. Hogue wouldn't begrudge her a biscuit from the tin of leftovers she'd seen sitting on the sideboard this morning. She'd ask.

However, when Dorrie reached her apartment, Mrs. Hogue's lamp was out and all was quiet, thus relegating Dorrie to her anteroom without nourishment. The lack of food intensified her headache.

She knelt beside her cot and prayed; she prayed more fervently than she had ever prayed in all her lifetime. She pleaded with heaven that she might find her grandparents. Then she lay a long while before the pain at the back of her neck eased enough to let her rest.

Sometime in the ebony night Dorrie awoke with a start. A choking atmosphere blanketed her room so thickly and heavily as to have substance. She coughed to clear her dry, sleep-lined throat. What had awakened her?

A piercing scream ripped the air, bringing her bolting upright. The wind came in gusts against the house, and then the shriek came again, a woman's high-pitched scream, followed by a sudden and sinister hush. Dorrie groped for the door.

"Mrs. Hogue! Mrs. Hogue!" She pounded with her fists on the wall while her heart thumped audibly against her ribs.

"What is it, Miss Taylor?" a sleepy voice asked.

"The scream—?"

"It is a cougar, Miss Taylor. Please calm yourself and let me get some sleep. If I must baby-sit a grown girl, I will be obliged to charge a higher fee."

Dorrie crept back to bed and lived the rest of the night wide-eyed to its end. The cat's cry had reduced her to a quivering mass of nerves.

Her insomniac thoughts skittered about from the past to the future with a confusing lack of demarcation. Where had her happiness ended and her restlessness begun? She'd had a lovely childhood with William and Nellie, a pleasant girlhood and an enjoyable adolescence. Then there had been the transition to young womanhood and the teaching job. Somewhere in her woolgathering, Gabriel intruded upon her thoughts along with his valiant effort to give her a set of last-minute guidelines.

She tried to reconstruct everything he had said because she needed it now. Tonight, the reassuring sense of protection that she had felt in the Harris unit was gone, replaced with a ghastly space, an awful detachment in this flat, inhospitable land.

Light was mantling the desert when Dorrie dressed

for the day. Dawn, which she trusted to bring composure, left her mind as disordered as the bed where she had tossed and turned in the aftermath of exhaustion.

Her head still hammered, and a dull weariness, compounded of tension and lack of sleep, tried to drag her down just when she needed to keep going. Her first priority was to obtain food. To her chagrin, she found that Mrs. Hogue wasn't home and no bread was left on the shelf. That meant that any comestibles must be obtained at the dingy restaurant with its disheveled chef. The prospect repulsed Dorrie.

Wind freighted with heavy sand met her when she stepped outside. Thin sheets of glasslike particles blew low: rising, whipping, falling, sweeping. The shifting dust shrouded far landmarks; she shielded her eyes against its assault, like daggers thrown at her face.

By walking part of the way backward to fend off the sally, she made it to the cafe. Most of the customers in the eatery were dusty-booted men with large, red noses and ruthless jaws. One of them gave a low whistle, and although she didn't know whether or not it was directed toward her, the thought crimsoned her face.

The proprietor gave her a taciturn nod and pointed a stubby finger toward a table at one end of the room. How would she be able to eat with the unsatisfied eyes of so many men upon her? She moved her chair so that her back would be to them.

The owner, rolled in a grimy cook's apron, brought her a glass of lukewarm water. It smelled even worse than its medicinal taste, but she drank it. "And whut kin I cook fur you?" he asked, his mouth full of something black that sloshed out the corners. He rolled back his lips when he talked, and his volume was louder than necessary.

"What have you to offer, sir?" Dorrie asked.

Several of the eavesdropping customers chortled. "Roadrunner, desert rats, or bobcat," one of them piped up. "Fried in snake oil."

"Excuse the manners of these *boys*, miss," the cook apologized, emphasizing the word "boys" to make the men look small. "You won't find much refinement in here. I do batch up a good griddlecake thut I serve with honey. My speshulty."

Dorrie's natural aversion to filth almost took her out the door from whence she had entered, but her ravenous appetite held her. "I'll take it, please," she nodded. "And a glass of milk."

"Goat's milk is all I have. But it's fresh."

Dorrie's stomach heaved. "That will be fine."

With her mind on eggs and ham, she ate doggedly through two griddlecakes, surprised at their tastefulness. They might not have much food value, but they were pulp for her hunger pains.

Before she'd finished her meal, Mrs. Hogue came rushing in, out of breath. "Mariposa Carrow is dead, York," she panted. "Sheriff Dodd found her on the floor in front of her cook stove this morning. He had gone to confiscate some of her records. And get this: the bellicose old soul had stuffed those records in the stove and burned them to cinders! How she ever got a fire going in that wheezy old range nobody knows. She hadn't the strength to lift a stick."

"She and Dodd've been arguing over those outdated papers fur years." The man called York grinned. "And I'd say she outfoxed him. In fact, I've never seen anybody

Mariposa Carrow *didn't* outfox unless it was the devil himself."

Mrs. Hogue spotted Dorrie sitting in the corner. "Oh, Miss Taylor," she effused, "I do regret that your sleep was disturbed last evening. Sometimes a cat cries when there's a death. Or maybe the screech was old lady Carrow's soul being dragged away by the demons. Who knows? If there was ever a wicked woman, it was she.

"But now that she is gone, you might be able to rent her house. That is, if you're not afraid of the spirit of the unredeemed dead. It is a solid shanty, except for the leaky roof, and with a bit of cleaning—" She stopped, voicing second thoughts, "Of course, I'd hate to lose you as a renter."

"Thank you, Mrs. Hogue, but I didn't come to make my home in Seminole. I will be leaving shortly—on the next northbound stage, in fact."

"That'll be three more weeks, miss," one of Mr. York's listening clients informed. "And the stage only goes east and west from here. There are no north and south connections. You'll be obliged to head east back to Lubbock and connect northward there. It's miles out of the way and time eating, but it's your only hope of getting that direction from Seminole."

"I thought Miss—that is, I thought someone said a wagon went from here to Amarillo."

"That's a *supply* wagon, miss," Mr. York explained. "It's an old buckboard that isn't passenger worthy. We send for supplies four times a year."

"When—when is it going?"

"When I get all the lists turned in. Probably in the next week or so."

"Is it safe?"

"It's never been robbed yet."

"I mean, would it be safe for a woman?"

"For a woman?"

"A passenger. Me."

"Depending on the driver, I 'spect," drawled one of the crusty patrons.

"I wouldn't recommend that you go by wagon," Mr. York said. "The drivers couldn't stop for your convenience or comfort. It's a through-fast trip. The vehicle goes empty, which makes it an uncomfortable old bucket, and there's no protection from wind or sun. You'd best wait for the coach and take the long way home."

"If I can be sure that I will not be harmed by unprincipled men, I would like to go along, please. I will cause the driver no inconvenience, and I will pay. I—I need to get there—to my family—as soon as possible. It is urgent."

"I'll drive, boss," volunteered a gimlet-eyed fellow with a camel-shaped face.

"I will send a *trustworthy* driver, John," rebuked Mr. York, giving the speaker a look that squelched any ambitions he might have had. He turned to Dorrie. "Be ready to travel next week, miss."

Thus began the longest week of Dorrie's life. Now she had more than one reason for wanting to make a speedy exit. *She* knew how Miss Carrow had accomplished her last "impossible" feat and who had fed the stove and provided the fuel for the destruction of the documents. No one must learn that she was the unwitting accomplice!

On Sunday, she attended a small church with Mrs. Hogue, but the congregation had a different concept of

God from what she had been taught. They recited memorized prayers in a monotone and talked more about their founder, a man whose name Dorrie had never heard, than of the Builder and Maker of the New Jerusalem. Their unfamiliar hymns were sung without spirit.

"We just stay with the church so that we'll have someone to marry our young and bury our dead," supplied Mrs. Hogue. "It's a habit I've tried not to break over the years though I think I could make better use of my time."

When Dorrie mentioned real and heartfelt salvation, the woman waved her hand to shoo away the idea. "We're not religious out here," she said. "It won't do any good to try to change us. Once a tight-minded sect tried to come in, and we ran them out of town. We live by our own notions and die by them. After living out here in no man's land, I figure we'd never be comfortable in heaven anyhow."

That night, Dorrie wept. She wept for the lost Miss Carrow, for the misguided Mrs. Hogue, and for all the bereft souls who existed on this margin of civilization. She would never have admitted to homesickness, but she yearned for the sound of Nellie's voice, the touch of her hand. She missed William and Billy, too. She should write, but to write would unleash the savage ache that she tried to hold at bay. She dare not give her emotions their head.

When she had another love, a new family to replace the one she'd left behind, it would be easier. . . .

CHAPTER 7

# Nellie's Mission

"Sometimes it seems but a few days since our Dorrie left, and sometimes it seems like gray centuries." Nellie Harris's hands slipped from her eyes to expose them wide and filmed with tears. How could she come to grips with this agonizing emptiness? "If only she would write!"

Nellie had spent much time in prayer, but her nerves refused to calm. When she thought of Dorrie's going away, every fiber in her body came to life, whimpering at the onset then roaring in protest. What right had another family to claim her daughter, enjoy her, possess her when they had no part in the anguish and ecstasy of her rearing? How could a father who had carelessly abandoned her trump up a solicitude he had forfeited years ago?

Her thoughts traveling a road of many switch backs, Nellie wept her way into Dorrie's room. The wind billowed the south window's curtains, permitting a piercing ray of sunlight to point a ghostly finger toward the hand-drawn picture on the wall. It was Dorrie's initial attempt at art, a first-grade revelation of the child's astonishing ability with crayons. She had sketched the family dog. "Why, I'd recognize that dog on a U.S. marshal's poster," avowed William.

On the armoire sat a picture of Billy. Dorrie had captured the boyishness of his face and the manliness of his eyes. Golden lights played in his rich chestnut hair.

It seemed to Nellie that her daughter had spent the bulk of her life with smudges of paint on her nose. She posed her dolls and painted them: sitting at a tea table, saying their prayers, tucked in bed. Once she sat in front of the mirror and drafted her own reflection. *Dorrie. Oh, Dorrie . . .* When Nellie looked at the picture, so lifelike, gulping sobs drove her from the room.

William was a wise man. He gently suggested that Nellie find something to occupy her vacuous hours at this bleak watershed of her life. It would be better, he counseled, if she could get away from the house where memories burrowed.

His suggestion took Nellie to the newly built hospital as a volunteer. She especially liked the nursery, but the greater need was in the post-operative wing, where she changed bandages and made mending patients comfortable. This is where she met Mrs. Holt.

Nellie told William all about her patient. "I've never seen a woman with a more beautiful spirit nor one so patient in suffering," she reported. "When her pain becomes intolerable, she sings, quotes Bible verses, or praises God."

"How old is this woman?" William asked, relieved that Nellie's mind had found a diversion.

"Oh, I'd guess her to be about my age."

"And she had surgery?"

"Yes."

"She is recovering nicely?"

"No. She has a malignancy, and the doctor says that the operation was not successful. It is only a matter of time—probably a short time—and she will be gone. Yet it seems the closer Mrs. Holt gets to death, the happier she becomes."

"That's as it should be for a child of God. She knows that she is going to a better place."

"But how I will miss her! No longer than I have known her, she has become a dear friend. When I should be encouraging her, she lifts my spirits instead. I told her all about Dorrie and how lonely I have been since she left. She understands. She bade me put my daughter in God's hands and rest assured that everything will come out according to His divine plan. She urged me to release my fears and worries and to enjoy a freedom from the—the pain in my heart."

"Has she a family?"

"She has one son. He must be Dorrie's age. She's very proud of him. I haven't met him; he works on the farm in the daytime and sits the night with her. Leaving him behind is her only regret. He will be all alone."

"We've been known to adopt children before," mused William. "Perhaps we could be his second family."

"William! You are such a big-hearted man. I will assure Mrs. Holt that her son will always have a welcome in our home. I'm sure that will be a solace to her."

When Nellie returned to the clinic the following week, Mrs. Holt's condition had worsened; indeed, she grasped life by a mere thread. The doctor handed Nellie a sheet of hastily drawn directions to Mrs. Holt's home and asked if she would go for the dying woman's son.

Nellie found the young man hoeing cotton. As she started across the patch toward him, he threw down the hoe and met her on the run. "Is it my mother, ma'am?" he asked.

"Yes, Mr. Holt. She is very low, and the doctor sent me to fetch you to the hospital."

He dusted the silt from his overalls and followed Nellie to the car. "I hope that I'm not too dirty—?"

"No. Please get in. I'm afraid that we've no time to lose."

Should she leave or stay in the room and witness the anguish of a mother and son's parting? Nellie bowed her head as the young man held his mother's frail hand and talked to her. He thanked her for the brave little soldier she had been and promised to meet her in heaven "just inside the eastern gate." When she drew her last breath, he gently kissed her cheek and folded her hands across her breast. Only when she had gone from his hearing did he give way to a spasm of weeping.

When Nellie tried to offer sympathy, he gave her a radiant smile through his tears. "She is in a better place," he said. "I would not call her back. Her life was not easy. The rest she gets is overdue. Anyway, I shall see her again."

William and Nellie attended Mrs. Holt's funeral then joined the mourners at the church afterward for a meal provided by the parishioners. William invited Mrs. Holt's son to visit them.

"I will do that, sir," promised the young man, "as soon as the farm chores give me the leisure."

"Your name is Gabriel?"
"Yes, sir, but most people call me Gabe."

CHAPTER 8

# A Place Called Tulia

The hours stretched long and the days hot. Dorrie lowered her bonnet over her eyes, wondering whether the heat it generated was worth the shade. She had asked for no favors, occasioned no unnecessary stops for the wagon driver, and yet there was something about him that made her feel that he resented her presence.

He sat in his seat with unmoving steadiness, his left hand resting on the wooden edge of the wagon and his right hand holding the reins. For miles neither he nor the scenery changed. The great reaches ahead led endlessly onward through the deceiving distance. Infrequently, they crossed a dry wash.

Dorrie propped her back against her portmanteau and observed nature in its most awful attire: a spider web of earth, cut and looped into drab ridges of rust and brown. It was both awesome and repulsive. Here and there, the bare clay was dotted with rocks and scant brush, a graveyard for plants, animals, and humanity.

To conclude the first day, they stopped in a place called Brownfield where Dorrie lodged with an already overburdened family. She slept with two of the younger children. The second night was spent in Midland, where the accommodations were better but the fare worse. The driver took orders along the way, which slowed their progress. Dorrie decided that this sideline business was a secret enterprise of an unscrupulous coachman, accounting for his churlish disposition.

Little bothered Dorrie now. The contemplation of journey's end brought with it a forbearance that had not been hers earlier. By the third night, they had reached Plainview, and the driver promised that the next day would take them to Tulia, a small town from which she would travel to Tule Canyon on her own. His route took him farther north to Amarillo, and he hadn't the time to go out of his way.

Tulia consisted of a few random buildings leaning windward and a courthouse. The inconsiderate chauffeur, eager to be on his way to make an extra dollar, deposited her luggage on the flagstone steps of the courthouse and disappeared in a whirlwind of dust. He didn't bother to look back.

Dorrie supposed she'd have to walk to Tule Canyon, but upon asking a passerby the distance there, she learned that it was twenty miles. She could never manage her trunk that far. She had money, though, and money talked. She would hire a liveryman if need be.

She could tell by the ruddy, darkening west that it was growing late. The daylight wouldn't hold for long. It would be better to wait, to rest until morning. She needed to allow her spirit to rebound, to have a bath and wash her hair, before meeting her grandparents.

The bewhiskered judge came bustling from the city hall and eyed her as though she had done something dreadfully wicked. "If you are a tramp waiting to be picked up, girl, I'll ask that you move on. Soliciting is not allowed here."

Dorrie's dark, proud eyes and mute lips refuted his insinuation. In that brief moment, anger somersaulted through her, leaving her pale and shaken. How dare he!

The shock that rippled across her face and the tears she pinched back had an effect on the man. "Where are you from and where are you going?" he demanded, but his voice had lost its sting.

"I'm Dorrie Harris from Cleburne, sir, and I've traveled many miles to see my grandparents, Slocum and Iantha Dorris, who live in Briscoe County. At least, that was their last known address. I came this far on an Amarillo-bound supply wagon. I have my own money, and I—I need to find a room for tonight. Then I'll hire someone to take me on to Tule Canyon tomorrow."

The judge jerked a thumb to indicate a location across the street where a low building sought the dignity of height with a false wooden front rising from its single story. "They've rooms over there for travelers. Costs a bundle, but it's the only place for a *decent* girl." The word he underscored with his voice, Dorrie gathered, was his way of righting his earlier inference. Then in a surprising gesture, he picked up her trunk and leaped toward the hotel without turning around to see whether or not Dorrie followed. He was gone when she arrived, and when Dorrie tried to pay, the clerk said the bill had already been taken care of. The judge's repentance covered that expense.

Bath water cost five cents, but Dorrie felt better when her body was cool and clean again. She rinsed out her stockings and hung them to dry before she dropped onto the bed, helpless with fatigue. The freshness of the evening air, blowing in the open window, immediately acted as a sedative to envelop her in needed hours of uninterrupted sleep.

A buttery morning light awoke Dorrie. She felt refreshed, tingling with a new thrill of anticipation, a feeling that all the tortuous miles of the past would soon be rewarded. Today she would meet her beloved grandparents. She dressed hurriedly, coiling her hair into a smooth chignon, anchoring it with her favorite silver comb. Ringlets played rebelliously about the nape of her neck. A quick consultation with the mirror satisfied her.

She made her way to the desk to ask about transportation to Tule Canyon. Her brain throbbed with a pulsating vibrancy. The culmination of her dreams lay before her, the nightmares of her investigation behind her.

The beak-nosed man at the counter was too busy to look up, and when he did, Dorrie saw that his eyes were hard. "Yes?"

"I need to hire a cart to take me to Tule Canyon today," she said, trying to regain some of the poise she'd lost to the man's abrupt manners and avaricious mien.

He analyzed her then licked his lips. "Transportation on the cap rock is very expensive," he said. "No one has time to drop what he is doing for a pleasure trip."

"I understand, and I am prepared to pay whatever the cost. The trip is most imperative."

"That will be four dollars."

*Four dollars!* That was more than a week's salary!

Dorrie heard a small gasp and thought it came from herself until she looked around. A plainly clad woman stood beside her. "Miss, we're going that direction and will be glad to give you a lift for free."

Not willing to lose the easy money, the man pursued. "What is the purpose of your going?"

"I am in search of my grandparents."

"And in the event that you don't find them, you will need a way back, won't you?" he was quick to reason. "The fare I quoted is round trip."

Dorrie turned to the woman. "Will you be returning?"

"Not for several weeks. But I'm sure—"

"What is the name of your relatives?" The rapacious man commandeered the conversation, and his pointed questions verged on rudeness. "My son travels widely. He might know your grandparents personally. If so, he could deliver you to their door."

"The name is Dorris. Slocum Dorris."

"Knight!" the man bellowed. "Do you know a Slocum Dorris in Tule Canyon?"

A young man appeared as if by magic. His glossy black hair was parted neatly in the middle; a single lock fell into a curl over his forehead. At a glance, Dorrie found him decidedly handsome and well-groomed. Seeing Dorrie, he gave an acknowledging bow.

"Why, yes, Father. Mr. Slocum is one of our suppliers. He runs the wholesale store near Silverton," Knight answered.

"This young lady is kin to Mr. Dorris. Get her there."

"Yes, sir."

Dorrie, still undecided, turned to the woman who had offered her the ride. "When will you be leaving, ma'am?"

"As soon as my husband gets the wagon hitched up."

"Just for you, we will drop the price, miss." The man placed both hands flat on the counter as if he planned to vault over. He pushed his head forward and lowered his voice for effect. "For two dollars you can go in style. You must consider that you are going to visit prominent members of a community, and you will wish to make a good impression. Knight will provide a surrey with a fringed canopy so that you will have shade all the way. He can be ready in a quarter of an hour. He will escort you to the door of the Dorris establishment in an amazingly short time. I assure you the luxury will be worth the investment."

Dorrie faltered, and the woman saw that she vacillated. "We—we haven't much to offer but dust and discomfort, I'm afraid," she acquiesced. "And our wagon will be much slower."

The price of two dollars was an exorbitant amount for carfare. Yet as difficult as it was to wrestle a decision from the unstable condition of her mind, Dorrie did wish to arrive looking fresh—and at the earliest possible moment. She reasoned that she could economize elsewhere.

"I believe I'll go with Mr. Knight." She gave the lady a smile of thanks.

Knight hurried away.

"Knight will collect your luggage, miss. We do everything first class," the man across the barrier said. "But we do require pay in advance." Dorrie dipped into her handbag and counted out two dollars.

When Dorrie saw Knight's rig, she drew in her breath in disbelieving delight, glad of her choice. It was the most beautiful horse car she had ever seen. The wheels and the running gear were scarlet, and the box, a luscious blue, was striped and scrolled with ruby. There were curlicues of gold on the hubs of the hickory wheels. An overlay of varnish made the whole thing resplendent. Two people could sit on the cushioned spring seat, and the coach sported a hard-topped roof with heavy curtains that could be lifted or lowered to suit the weather.

Knight took her hand and helped her aboard, making her feel like royalty. If this was a preview of what lay ahead, it was the prelude to a perfect day!

## Chapter 9

# Journey's End

Dorrie's gaze followed the sandy road as it wound out of sight across a prairie that stretched broad and limitless. Here the sand looked white; in the horizon it appeared red. Somewhere ahead were her people, her link to a brotherhood of flesh and blood. Cleburne and her past seemed a planet away.

"Will you work in the store?" Knight asked her.

"If they need me," she answered, blushing prettily. "I shouldn't like to be idle. Or a burden."

"How long will you visit?"

"I may make my home with my grandparents."

"Good. Then perhaps I could call on you now and then?"

She was both flattered and disturbed. "That would be nice, but I—I don't know you."

"Then we must remedy that, mustn't we?" His eyes, a dancing blue, gave Dorrie the sensation of going down a steep hill too fast.

At noon, Knight brought the surrey to a standstill near a beautifully ribbed and scalloped sand dune. He alighted and helped Dorrie down. Then from behind the seat he produced a picnic basket and a blanket. "If you will spread our lunch, I will check on our steed," he said. "And then we'll get better acquainted. You might find that you need a friend in this lawless country."

While he watered the horse from a bucket he had stored in the feed box, Dorrie arranged the goodies from the basket on a flat rock: fry bread, ham, pickles, new potatoes, mincemeat pie, and a jar of lemonade.

"You brought along quite a feast!" she laughed, truckling to the festivity of the occasion and her own excitement.

"It's Dad's way," Knight demurred. "My father is a politician, and he has to do everything magnanimously. Myself, I'd be satisfied with bread and butter. But do tell me about yourself. I've never seen you at your grandparents' store. You must not visit often."

"I have never met them," confessed Dorrie, her reticence sliding away. "Actually, I'm not sure they know that I even exist."

"At any rate, Mr. Dorris hasn't mentioned a granddaughter." Knight speared a pickle with his pocketknife. "Is there any particular reason for this enigma?"

"Yes. My mother was married to Slocum Dorris's son for a brief time. She had the marriage annulled when he left her. I'm not certain that my father knew that he had a daughter."

"To have so lovely a daughter and not know it would be most unfortunate."

"I understand that he is deceased."

"Yes, Mr. Dorris told me that he had three children but that his son was dead. The other two are girls. He mourns the death of his only son yet. I'm sure Mrs. Dorris will be especially delighted to learn that she has a granddaughter since her daughters bore sons," he made a sound that resembled a tired sigh, "and no-account ones at that. I hope those boys give you no trouble."

"The daughters and their sons—do they live nearby?"

"They're all in the business together. It is a family business."

"I see."

After their repast, they traveled again. By mid afternoon they reached a deep vee of a canyon where a ribbon of water meandered through the gulch, its stimulus evident. Knight pointed toward a covey of buildings that loomed in the distance. "Yonder is Silverton. It's about two miles farther on." He drew the carriage up flush with a long, two-sectioned structure. Pinioned by a metal wall bracket hung a sign that said DORRIS GENERAL STORE. "This is your grandfather's store. Shall I go in with you?"

"No, please. Just deposit my trunk at the door."

A scowling boy appeared, wearing the scorn of a fractious adolescent. He was tall and rawboned, and Dorrie guessed him to be about Billy's age. When he moved, he appeared to prowl. "We didn't order that, Knight," he barked when Knight deposited the suitcase near the entryway. "And Grandpa said we aren't doing any more trading."

"That matter will be between you and my passenger, Duff," Knight snapped. "I was paid properly to deliver her and her baggage to this location." He turned on his heels and started back toward the surrey.

The conversation brought an older man, a thin, used-up man with sparse hair and a red face who seemed scared, bounding to the door. "What's the problem, boys?"

"No problem, sir," Knight said. "Good day." He was gone, and suddenly Dorrie wished she could call him back. The environment here wasn't friendly. She'd stepped out of a storybook world into reality.

As she approached the store's entrance, the man stepped aside to allow her passage. The boy would have blocked her way had not the man given his arm a jerk. It was evident that they supposed her a buyer and that Duff didn't like women customers.

Gradually, Dorrie's eyes adjusted to the dim interior of the shop where merchandise littered the room. Horseshoes, nails, rope, and groceries cohabited in a jungle of disarray. How could anyone run a store with such blatant disorganization?

"May I help you, lady?" the man inquired.

"Sir, I'm looking for a Mr. Slocum Dorris."

"You're looking at Mr. Slocum Dorris." His air held a guarded suspicion. "Who are you, and why are you looking for me?" He seemed to expect Dorrie to challenge him on some issue of his commerce that he had already prepared himself to disprove.

The incongruity of the situation struck Dorrie, and she laughed aloud. Here she stood face to face with her own grandfather, and he had no idea who she was. He thought her a shopper. *Her grandfather!* She stepped forward, her face lit with an eager smile. "I am Susan Dorris, daughter of your son, Charles. He was married to my mother, Mattie Taylor—"

Mr. Slocum whitened about the mouth, swaying back and forth with one motion. "*Charles?* My son, Charles? But he is dead." He ran nervous fingers through the thin spatter of hair. "And you say—you say you are his *daughter*?"

"Yes, he wed my mother more than twenty years ago. They lived in Seminole—"

"How can I know that you speak the truth? That this is not a—a—?"

"I've come here from Seminole, Grandfather. I found my father's records there; they led me to you."

"Charles once mentioned a wife, but he didn't mention a daughter."

"He was probably unaware of my birth. He left my mother, and when he didn't return, she terminated the marriage and gave me her maiden name."

The old man's hands still shook pathetically. "And after all these years . . . you found me?"

"I found you, Grandfather." She reached out to touch his arm, and he didn't withdraw.

"And what about your mother?"

"She's dead, too."

"And you've come to—to live with us?" Dorrie couldn't tell whether he was pleased or displeased, but his speech stumbled on. "Iantha will be glad. Oh, she will be *so glad*! Duff, bring Susan's trunk in. I did get the name right, didn't I?"

"I've gone by Dorrie most of my life."

"Dorrie? Then let's leave it at that."

The boy's face darkened into disgust, and bitter derision curled his lips. "Spoiled rotten city girl," he muttered, and Slocum Dorris, his hearing shorted by age, didn't hear him. Dorrie did. She'd have her work cut out to win him over she judged, but it wouldn't take long. She had a way with boys. He would be great company, assuaging her homesickness for Billy.

"Duffy, you stay with the store, and I'll take Dorrie over to the house to meet Iantha," her grandfather directed. He turned to Dorrie. "I hope that your coming will cheer your grandmother. She hasn't been well of late."

*I've found them.* A gladness seized Dorrie, almost choking off her breath. The reception wasn't the rhapsody she had imagined, but she didn't have to have quick results. She just had to know her direction was right. It was enough to know that she had found her roots. In the lineage of Dorrises she would now take her place.

## Chapter 10

# Problems

Iantha Dorris cried when she learned that she had a granddaughter. She cried when Dorrie hugged her. She cried often and with little provocation, her tears gushing like a fountain in full play. She had been ill since Charles died, she claimed.

She had never been blessed with anyone to assist her with her housework; her own daughters pitifully neglected her. Ghastly headaches victimized her. She said she hoped that Dorrie would stay to love them and to help them. Dorrie's mind leaped to the challenge. She was needed, and she was wanted!

The place was a mess. How long had it been since this house had been thoroughly cleaned? No wonder her grandmother was sickly! Germs romped in this grime-encrusted site that smelled of stale food, human perspiration, and dirt. Her first priority must be to scrub the area from stem to stern and then get sufficient light and air into all the rooms.

Habits of tidiness and neatness would bring about a transformation after a while. Gabe had said she mustn't expect too much too soon. *A little at a time . . .*

Dorrie determined to sacrifice herself, giving all her time and strength to help these dear people. William's philosophy declared that no one could be truly great until he loved enough to forget his own self-interest. God had sent her here for a purpose, and she would fulfill that purpose if she had to forfeit everything except the hope of heaven.

The cupboards, nothing more than unpainted apple crates nailed to the wall, displayed chipped cooking pots and dishes. *Everything* was cracked or broken. The sink, with a short pipe that dumped water into a slop pail beneath, was old and stained. In the stead of a water pump, a granite dipper handle protruded from a blue-flecked bucket. The floor was bare, the walls paved with greasy and splattered oilcloth through which some of the wooden slats showed.

For her room, Iantha gave Dorrie the west ell, an added eyesore to the main body of the building. Though cramped, it had a window that opened out upon the sage country. Dorrie made immediate plans to get a new curtain to replace the tattered, sun-faded one that was shredded to ribbons at the bottom.

There was no rushing river here in Tule Canyon like the mighty Brazos, no oak trees, and no evergreens like those on Grandmother Harris's farm. On the other hand, Bosque County could boast no glorious sage blooming with opal fire at sunset. Nature had a way of balancing the books, reconciling the debits and credits.

Iantha began to ply for information about Dorrie's

past. What had her life been like with her adoptive parents? How large was their house? Were they prosperous? How long had she taught school? Her itch for any enlightenment in connection with Dorrie's childhood begged scratching.

Dorrie used caution in discussing the years spent with William and Nellie. It would be heartless to tell Iantha about Nellie's beautiful home since Iantha had not enjoyed such a lifestyle. Iantha didn't have the friends or a caring family that had been Nellie's luxury. If Dorrie painted glowing word pictures of her past, it might seem to Iantha that she was criticizing their simple way of life, and the last thing she wished to do was bring further distress to her sick grandmother.

As soon as she'd settled into her room, Dorrie spread her stationery on a wooden crate, placing her pen and ink beside it. She had promised to write to her mother (and to Billy), and she was eager to keep that commitment now that she had found her paternal grandparents and had some good news to share. Wouldn't they be delighted to learn that her travels had ended on a happy note? She would tell Billy that she had boy cousins about his age; she hadn't met them all yet. She would let Nellie know that she was needed here, thank her for the wonderful years of training, and inform them that she planned to remain with the Dorrises for an indefinite period of time.

Words spawned other words as she wrote. She described the store, the purple sage, and Knight's carriage. It was a heartwarming letter, and when she read it over, she realized that she had glossed over the travail that had brought birth to her new life. That was as it should be. She was an adult now, able to bear her own pain without bringing concern to others. She stamped and sealed her letter, satisfied with its contents.

Before the busy week was out, Iantha's daughters came by for a fleeting visit. Mary, the oldest, was short and chunky with a pushed-in face saved from homeliness by a bright pair of eyes. She pulled Dorrie aside and whispered in her ear, "We hope that you can help our mother. She has a problem that neither Lottie nor I know how to handle. She seems . . . better since you came. Tonight is the first time I've heard her laugh in months."

Dorrie hugged the idea to herself that she was responsible for Iantha's happiness, and after her aunts had gone, she sat down for a protracted visit with this grandmother of whom she had been deprived. "Tell me all about my father, about his sisters, and about my cousins," she pressed. "I am anxious to learn my history."

"Charles was twenty-two years old when he was killed," Iantha said, dabbing away tears.

"If talking about him is too painful—" Dorrie objected.

"No, you have a right to know. We never got the straight of what happened, Slocum and I. Some said he was drowned; some said he died of a fever. Since we didn't know where his body was put to rest, we erected a headstone here for memories. We'll take you to see it.

"You don't bear much favor to Charles except your eyes; I can see Charles there. I've forgotten so much of Charles's boyhood. He left home young, and his going seems a thousand ages ago. I'm sorry I can't tell you more.

"Mary was next born. She married at sixteen and has three boys: Duffy, Neal, and Jed. Duffy's the oldest. Her husband ran off to California three years ago and has never returned. Mary pretty well lets the boys do as they please. Slocum supports the whole passel with the profits from the store. Mary has no pity for my headaches; she's always favored her daddy.

"Lottie would've made a good daughter if it hadn't been for Mary's influence. Mary soured her against me. Lottie has a soft heart and a mean man. She has two boys. Slocum supports them, too.

"I don't need Mary so badly now that you've come, and I could tell today that she was jealous. The girls probably think you've showed up to claim your part of the inheritance. But I can tell you, the more you try to grab, the less you'll get."

"Oh, Grandmother Dorris!" protested Dorrie, making a wall of her hands. "I didn't think of money when I came. I don't need anything. I have my own money, and I can make a good living with the education that I have. I've come to be a blessing not a burden. Please make that clear to your daughters!"

"I know, but *they* don't know. I will try to make them understand."

"Grandmother Dorris, are you and Grandfather Christians?"

Iantha gave her a strange, unreadable look. "Our lifestyle and church don't mix, Dorrie."

"But, Grandmother, salvation is life's most important commodity!"

"If you stay long enough, you'll learn that around here that is not so."

"Oh, Grandmother! *Please* don't say that!"

Not only was Iantha's body sick, but so was her soul. A crushing weight fell upon Dorrie's spirit. Could she lead her family to Jesus? She must! She would stay and try until all possibilities had been exhausted or circumstances sent her away.

She tacked an addendum to Nellie's letter asking her mother to join her in prayer for this miracle. Slocum Dorris said he would see that the letters were mailed the next day. Duff would be making a trip to the post office.

Dorrie also needed a bottle of bluing and a box of starch. She asked if Duff wouldn't mind picking up those items for her while he was in town. The two-dollar carriage fare had depleted her purse change, so she went to her trunk for money to purchase the supplies.

However, when she opened her luggage, she found the contents in disarray and the money gone. Every penny of it.

# Chapter 11

# Bonding

Through the cracks of grief, Gabriel Holt's loneliness grew with tenacious vigor. It sprouted, pushing its way to the surface despite his efforts to keep it contained beneath the hard crust of self-control.

He missed his mother, but the strongest pain would always be associated with his schoolteacher, Dorrie Harris. He supposed that every boy in the class was in love with her as a matter of principle, but she did not encourage their attention. She had a fetching face, yet she was far from vain.

Gabriel recalled everything incident to the last talk they'd had: her long, tapered fingers, the graceful way she held her head, the burnished gold of her hair in the shadows, the dark lashes that swept to copper-hued tips, and the tone of her voice. Miss Harris could bring warmth to the coldest of hearts.

Each word she had spoken had thrilled him, as well as the way she had looked into his eyes, directly and with girlish innocence. He told himself he must not read too much into that one tryst, but what harm could come of dreaming?

She was gone, but her gestures, her smile, her charm were ghosts that glimmered about his mind every day, beckoning to him. No one would ever fill her place in his heart.

When the canker of isolation reached Gabriel's spirit and began eating away there, he remembered the invitation of a man who had attended his mother's funeral. He thought his name was Williams. Mr. Williams had a son, he said, embarking on the turbulent teenage years, who was trying to adjust to the loss of a sister. Since Gabe had lost a mother, he might be able to help a boy who had suffered a bereavement also. After all, he did owe something to the lady who had contributed so much of her time to befriending his mother in her ebbing days. Propriety demanded that he respond.

On this premise, one afternoon in late August, Gabriel followed the map that William had drawn for him to the Harris homestead, where Nellie welcomed him with warm solicitude. The smell of fresh bread pleased his nose while arousing his stomach. He had not tasted homemade bread since before his mother's last sick spell.

"Make yourself comfortable," Nellie offered. "My husband and son will be in from the blacksmith shop any minute."

Gabriel sat in the porch swing and watched the shade crawl across the ground, jotting down meditative notations of his surroundings. The house stood in a circle of post oak trees, green and gold and smelling deeply of summer. A spring-fed pond lay beyond the trees, no small item in the property's value. Morning glories swarmed over the fence, their pods asleep for the day.

Mr. Williams kept a neat outlay. The shrubs were manicured, the outbuildings recently painted, and the fences in good repair. The place was peaceful and harmonious, the effect of a diligent man.

Glancing up, Gabe noticed that clouds clustered in gray and black formations, swallowing more and more of the sky. The atmosphere held its breath for a summer tantrum. Perhaps he should not have come, or perhaps he should rush away before the rain caught him and he became stranded. Yes, he decided, he should hurry back home. He started to the door to tell Nellie of his decision when William and Billy arrived.

"Oh, you must stay!" William insisted. "You can't do anything in the rain but sit inside alone, and you might as well be here with us. Billy will take you in a game of checkers after supper."

Billy grinned, and an unspoken friendship was born. Gabe stayed, assured that if he was at home the inner storm would out-rage the elements.

Nellie laid the long harvest table with an elaborate spread. She had made several kinds of pies and pressured Gabe to sample them all. "You'll have my clothes shrinking, Mrs. Nellie," he joked.

Gabriel was surprised at himself and a little frightened. He, who had never felt he belonged anywhere, felt at ease here. He had only been in the company of the Williamses a short while, yet they seemed more like family than mere acquaintances.

By the time the meal ended, the thunder banged about from the clouds overhead to those far away, chasing veins of fire across the sky. A cloudburst of solid water tumbled down, fostering a pleasant, sylvan smell.

"This is a welcome sight to a farmer, is it not, Gabriel?" William asked.

"Yes, sir. The Lord takes good care of His children."

William lit the lamps, and Billy brought the checkers. When William left them to their game, Billy spoke up, "I'm glad it's raining so you can't go home. It gets mighty lonesome around here since my sister is gone. She used to play checkers with me."

"I can't take her place, of course," remarked Gabe, "but I'm glad I can fill in the vacant spot. I'm not an expert, by any means."

"She was good at it! But sometimes I think she just *let* me win so I wouldn't get discouraged."

"How long has your sister been—" Gabriel started to say dead, but realized how final that sounded, so he changed his mind. "—gone?"

"About three months."

"It's hard to lose a dear one," Gabriel said. "I know how it feels." It might help Billy to talk about his sorrow. "But if she was a Christian, I'm sure she's happy where she is."

"Oh, she was a Christian, all right!" answered Billy. "She was the best Christian anywhere! She prayed every morning and every night and read her Bible, too. She read clean through the Bible *every year*! When I was just a wee lad, she would tell me the most wondrous Bible stories. Why, she could make those characters come alive in my mind and walk right off the pages!" Memory softened Billy's eyes.

"How old was she when she—went?"

"She was twenty, going on twenty-one."

"Did she go suddenly? Was it an—accident?"

"No, we knew that she was going a few weeks ahead of her leaving. Still, it seemed sudden when she finally left."

"I know. One is never ready for parting. I'm sorry."

"Winter will be the hardest, I think, when the days are dark and the nights long."

"Would it help if I come over now and then to take her place in a checker game?"

"Oh, it would help ever so much!" exploded Billy. "Would you really do that?"

"It might ease the pain of both of our losses."

Billy was a good player, an opponent who kept Gabe on his toes. He forgot the time in his preoccupation with the contest. The clock struck nine.

Gabe jumped to his feet. "I should have gone an hour ago," he apologized. "I'm afraid I've overstayed my welcome on the very first visit."

Billy laughed. "You can't go *anywhere*, Gabe. It's still raining cats and dogs."

"Billy is right," William agreed, joining them. "You'll be obliged to spend the night with us, Gabriel. There's a regular storm outside with not a hint of retreat. You've no one to worry over at home tonight, have you?"

"No, sir."

"Well, *we* would worry if you *did* return home."

"I wouldn't want to put you out."

"Gabriel, you are filling a cavity that has been hollow in our hearts for three months. If you wouldn't mind sleeping in our daughter's room—?"

"Oh, no, sir. Anywhere will be fine."

"It still has her girl-things in it." Billy wrinkled his nose. "And you're a *man*."

"So does my mother's room," Gabe nodded. "But it's reassuring to keep them there, isn't it?"

It was a strange feeling to be sleeping in a young lady's room, in her bed. Promptly, he blew out the lamp so that the feminine embellishments could not be seen. They reminded him of his art teacher, and if he put his mind on her, he would be awake all night.

About midnight, the rain halted, but the frogs sang discordantly for an encore. Hanging between deep sleep and a light doze, Gabriel conceded he wouldn't mind if it rained a week and trapped him here where smiles were plentiful and plates were full of a woman's cooking. What would it be like to be part of a family? An unfathomable craving ricocheted through his body; then the impression dimmed and he slept again.

Gabriel awoke to the smell of frying bacon. A rosy sunrise peeped over the window sill, muted by gauzy curtains. *Where am I?* He looked about the room, and the first thing he saw was the portrait that Dorrie had painted of herself. Miss Harris! His teacher! What was her picture doing in the Williams girl's room? Miss Harris had probably been her art instructor, too, he surmised. Or a good friend.

At breakfast, even the eggs and grits and boysenberry jelly could not hold Gabe's distracted mind. The portrait had kidnapped his attention. "Did you rest well, Gabriel?" Billy worried.

"Um, what did you ask, Billy? Oh, yes, thank you. I don't think I turned a corner all night," Gabe stuttered.

"That will be your room anytime it rains. Or snows.

Or ices. Or our checker game lasts too long," proffered the boy.

"Thank you."

"I hope you don't mind that it is a *girl's* room."

Could Gabe bring himself to ask about the picture, to tell them that their daughter's friend was his teacher? Would the pain of referring to her supersede the pain of silence? "The picture—?" he fumbled. "Of Miss Harris—"

"She painted it herself," bragged Billy. "She was an artist."

"Yes, I know. She was my art teacher. I was—older before I completed my education. She helped me to graduate."

"Dorrie was your art teacher?"

"Miss Harris, yes."

"My *sister*?"

"No, not your sister. Your sister's friend, Miss Harris."

"Dorrie Harris *is* my sister. Her name is really Susan, but we call her Dorrie. She went to search for her father's family—"

"Miss Harris? But—but I thought your name was Williams."

"Dad's name is William. William Harris. He and Mom adopted Dorrie and me when I was a baby."

Comprehension seeped into Gabe's befuddled mind in small increments. It was too much to absorb all at once. *I am a guest of Miss Harris's family. I slept in Miss Harris's room.*

Rationality forsook him. "It's—it's—what a surprise, but a wonderful one. Have—have you heard from her? Where is she?" he asked, babbling like a cretin.

"We haven't heard a word from her," Nellie spoke up.

"She promised to write, and it isn't like Dorrie not to keep a promise. I hope that she is well. And safe." Her voice broke.

Gabriel experienced a tumble in his diaphragm, a rise in his blood. His thoughts hopscotched over stones of anxiety. *What if she had gotten married?*

## Chapter 12

# A New Job

Had Dorrie entertained any hopes of returning to the refuge of her upbringing, those hopes were now dashed with the disappearance of her money. Finding the choice snatched from her, she thought of her former home even more often. For a week, she wrote to her parents every day and then awaited eagerly for the return mail. A month passed, but no letters came for her.

Unbeknown to Dorrie, Duff had not mailed her letters. He calculated that any word from her past life might lure her back, sabotaging his chances for more easy money in the future. He didn't like her, but he didn't want to lose any advantage for dishonest gain. She might come in handy. . . .

Duff loathed the way Dorrie rearranged his grandmother's house, making everything smell like soap. She was trying to change them all, to make them religious goody-goodies. The fancy food she cooked took a vast chunk of his grandfather's income. Besides, he had planned on occupying the room she took when school commenced again. Nobody rooted out Duff A. Costler without paying the penalty.

Iantha's health had improved considerably; a whole month elapsed without a headache. Mary was quick to give Dorrie credit for the improvement, expressing her sincere gratitude. She even said she hoped Dorrie would "stay forever." Dorrie, she maintained, had accomplished in a few days what the whole family had not been able to do in years. Slocum Dorris showed relief, too, in a detached fashion. He was seldom around. The business demanded his soul and body.

Dorrie didn't mention the loss of her money. She was reasonably sure that Duff had taken it since he was the one responsible for transporting her baggage, but to accuse him would mean alienating herself from her grandfather. The old man doted on Duff and would accept no disparagement of the boy's character. An indictment would be like blood in the water to a circling shark; they would all attack *her*.

Nor would Dorrie ask for charity. She needed thread to darn her stockings. She would simply post a notice in her grandfather's store for work as an artist to earn the funds for her small necessities.

However, when Dorrie took the advertisement to the store, a frown drew Slocum Dorris's salient eyebrows into mounds that mirrored his distaste for the idea. "Oh, no, Dorrie!" he said quickly. "Your grandmother needs you, and I wouldn't think of allowing you to work outside the home. It might be—dangerous to us all."

"Then perhaps I could paint at home and display my items here?"

He was shaking his head vigorously. "If you must work, I'll put you on at the store for a few hours a week."

"But I want my own spending money."

"I could pay you a small sum. I wouldn't want it said that Old Man Dorris couldn't care for his granddaughter."

Her grandfather's rationale made no sense to Dorrie, but that week she went to work in the store, clerking at the counter. Right away, she saw that much of the merchandise in stock was woefully outdated. Some of it, cosseted in dust or spider webs, hadn't been moved in months. She sold little, which was understandable. What woman would come two miles for a sack of weevil-infested cornmeal when she could buy it in town? It didn't add up. Why had her grandfather chosen such a remote site for a general store? And if she sold no more than this, how could he afford to pay her wages?

A booming business, though, took place in the feed store, a musty, foul-smelling room separated from the main framework by a roughly hewn wall. Men came and went, hauling away burlap bags and milk cans. Occasionally, one of the men wandered into her section of the store for coffee beans or sorghum. She dreaded male customers. Most of them tramped into her presence without removing their hats or showing a semblance of courtesy.

At the end of two weeks, Dorrie still hadn't seen a penny, and the hole in her hosiery spread like a disease. When she broached the subject of wages, her grandfather gave her a blank stare. "I gave Duff the money to pay you at the end of last week," he said. "Have you spent your salary already? I will ask you to be more thrifty, Dorrie."

"I prefer that you pay me directly, Grandfather," she requested.

"I don't see that it matters," he rebutted, "but if that's what it takes to make you happy—"

"Please," Dorrie nodded.

August stepped aside for September, and summer's heat began to lose its clout. Dorrie's sense of well-being felt bruised, and she tried to identify the source of her depression. Did she feel abandoned by her Harris family? Did she miss teaching school? Was she homesick? Were the adjustments here too stringent for her narrow, insulated life? She had promised herself that she would lead her grandparents to God if it took the rest of her life, and the battle had just begun. They knew so little about Him! She must not become discouraged at the beginning of the race. She would need to muster all her spiritual resources—

There! That was the problem! Her soul was dry and thirsty. She had not been to God's house for much too long. Without spiritual food, one's inner being waned just as a physical body became faint without natural food. If she hoped to impart strength to others, she must be strong herself. It was imperative that she find a church to attend, a parson to shepherd her.

Her grandmother's health began to deteriorate again. The headaches returned, and the more frequent the headaches the less attention Iantha's family paid her. Mary stopped coming by altogether. It was a puzzle Dorrie could not piece together.

Then one day as Dorrie returned from her fruitless stint at the store, she saw her grandmother behind the barn on her knees, scratching around in the sand. Thinking her ill, Dorrie ran to her. "Grandmother!" she cried. "Are you okay? Let me help you back to the house!"

Iantha jerked her head and looked at Dorrie through tortured eyes. "I'm—okay. I've been coming out here ever since Charles died."

"What are you doing on the ground?"

"I—I have his picture buried here. In a box. I dig it up ever so often. To help me remember. Oh, Dorrie, it's so hard!" She began to weep, her eyes shedding great crystal droplets. "You don't know. You don't understand. Oh, I hope that you never have to know!"

Dorrie knelt beside her grandmother and put her arms about her. "I'm sorry, Grandmother."

Iantha stiffened. "There's nothing you can do. Please go away and leave me alone. I don't like anyone watching me—grieve for Charles."

Dorrie backed away, her heart hammered and sore. She had been here a full three months, and yet she knew so little about her grandparents. They were still strangers, shuffling through life on a different strata.

What had Gabe said? *Your new family may not meet your expectations. You must not make comparisons. . . . They may not be Christians. . . . Give yourself room to adjust to them. . . . Take changes a little at a time. . . .* Thank you, Gabe. You were an oracle of God.

Dorrie knew what she must do, what she *would* do. Making a token stop at the house for her parasol, she set out on a walk to town to find a church. Without the support and fellowship of other believers, she couldn't survive.

Silverton was laid out in tic-tac-toe fashion with two main streets running east and west and two going north and south. From this center, the town crawled outward to residences and ranches. Finding the small adobe church was no problem; one inquiry took Dorrie there. The parson lived directly behind the sanctuary.

Celia Boston, the minister's wife, was at home, busy with her needlework for the poor. She showered Dorrie with such motherly kindness that Dorrie wavered precariously between tears and laughter. The woman reminded her of Nellie. In size. In looks. In attitude.

"My dear! You will find such a welcome here!" Celia beamed. "We are a small and struggling congregation, and another voice to join us in worship will be such a blessing!" She did not ask questions or probe into Dorrie's reason for coming. "My spirit gives witness that you are a child of God," she stated, "and that's all that matters.

"And are you musical? Someone donated a pianola to the church, but we've no one to play it."

"I play a little," was Dorrie's modest admission.

"How my husband will rejoice!" Celia bubbled. "He's been praying for a pianist. It's hard to strike the right key for the hymns a cappella."

Before Dorrie left the parsonage, she and Celia Boston knelt for a season of prayer together. A new resolve was born, and Dorrie basked in the sweet release it brought. She promised to attend the weekend church services.

The visit lasted longer than she had planned, necessitating a brisk walk to get her home in time to cook supper. About halfway to Tule Canyon, a fast-moving carriage passed her and then pulled up short, creating a fog of billowing dust.

"Miss Harris!" a congenial voice greeted. Dorrie recognized the set of hickory wheels with their gold ornamentation. Knight sprang from the driver's seat and offered his hand. "It will be my distinct honor to provide transportation for you to your destination, fair lady. And with no charge except your lovely presence."

Dorrie's heart gave an unexpected lurch. Such chivalry was a rare thing in this untamed land. She gave him her hand, and he helped her into the carriage.

## Chapter 13

# Ministering

Duff saw Knight and Dorrie pass the store and took the report straight to his grandfather's ears, embellishing the story to include other times Dorrie had "slipped off" with men. He was angry because Dorrie demanded her wages directly from Mr. Dorris's own hands. It had detoured his plans to keep part of it for himself.

The falsehood made Slocum angry. Dorrie had come to them like a lamb, but she had transmuted into a tigress beneath her mild manners and pseudo-righteousness. She would work long enough to get a little money—taking advantage of their goodness—and then run wild. No wonder Iantha was having her "spells" again; she knew what Dorrie was really like.

A fuming Mr. Dorris left the store in Duff's custody and headed straight home for a confrontation with his granddaughter. His arsenal of words was well stocked, his tongue loaded.

Iantha was abed in her room, sleeping off a sick

headache. That, Mr. Dorris figured, was in his favor. Dorrie had just donned her apron with the intentions of preparing a nutritious supper when her grandfather called her outside onto the front stoop.

"Where did you go today?" he asked, skewering her with cold, gray eyes.

"I walked to town to visit the parson's wife."

"Without asking Iantha's permission?"

"Grandmother requested that I leave her alone to—to grieve for her son. Besides, I'm celebrating my twenty-first birthday this month, and I'm not a child, Grandfather." Her chin went up with just a hint of stubbornness.

"You walked to town and walked back, eh?"

"No, sir. I walked to town and part of the way back. Knight, the gentleman who brought me here from Tulia, offered me a ride on home in his carriage."

"How long have you been slipping off?"

Dorrie was shocked. "I have never slipped off."

"Duff has seen you. Don't lie to me." His eyes flashed.

It was her word against Duff's. "I've been here for three months, Grandfather Dorris," she said, treading softly, "and I have gone nowhere except to the store. God is my witness." She put her elbow against the house to steady herself.

"Why did you feel it necessary to talk to the parson's wife? We settle our own problems within the family."

Dorrie took a deep breath. "I need a place to worship," she explained. "Attending church has always been an integral part of my life. My soul must have spiritual nourishment just like my body must have food—"

"And the first thing you know," bellowed Slocum, "some stodgy preacher will come poking his nose around my property wanting to convert me. I'll not have anyone snooping around—"

"These aren't nosy people, Grandfather. They're Christians."

"Christians, bah!" His utterance vibrated with venom. "I've had my worst troubles with holier-than-thous." He stopped, checking the slowly gathering might of his wrath. In a more reasonable tone, he continued, "Listen, Dorrie. We're glad you've come. You've done a heap for Iantha, and I'm glad to come home to a hot meal. But we're private people. We live our own lives and expect everyone else to do the same. That's our creed. I don't want you going off anywhere to church. Before you know it, those folks will try to wrangle their way into our business through you. You'll be their point of contact. I'm asking—no, I'm demanding that you not mingle with the population of Silverton."

Dorrie hoped the Lord would hear her unspoken entreaty. *Lord, what shall I do?* She hadn't the funds to return to her girlhood home, and they might not want her back anyway. She didn't wish to disobey her grandfather and cause problems here, but her soul was dying. She suffered. Hope drifted far away.

An idea—from whence did it spring?—came suddenly, forcefully. "Grandfather, I pray each evening, but the Bible says where *two or three* are gathered together, the Lord will be in their midst. If I cannot go to church, then I must insist that you and Grandmother have a time of devotion with me at least once a week."

"I—well—" Slocum was cornered, caught in his own trap. "What would we do at these—devotions?"

"We'll read the Bible and talk about God. And pray."

"All right." There was an odd subnote of resignation. "If that's what it takes to keep you out of town *and* if Iantha agrees. I will leave it up to her." He turned and hurried away.

Dorrie was jubilant. The victory had come so easily, so unexpectedly. *Some of life's greatest blessings rise from seeming defeat.* Gabe had said it, and how true that was! Her grandfather had made a concession toward religion. A small one, granted, yet it was a beginning. She had never imagined herself a missionary, but that thought brought joy to her heart, lightness to her feet. Hadn't Gabe said she must be patient? Gabe had said . . . Why was she thinking about Gabe?

By the following morning, Iantha's headache had worn itself out, and Dorrie approached her about a miniature service in their home. "We'll sing hymns and read from the Bible, and I'll try to answer any questions you and Grandfather might have," enthused Dorrie.

Iantha stifled a yawn. "Whatever you say, Dorrie. That might be fun. Can we have refreshments when we're finished? When I was young, we had refreshments at the end of every party. How about some of your good raisin shortbread?" Her lips wore the outline of a smile, but it was empty.

"Of course. In Bible times, the disciples broke bread together."

The first "service" was a bittersweet revelation to Dorrie. She learned that her grandparents knew nothing at all about God's Word. They knew nothing of Abraham or Joseph or Moses. They were ignorant of Peter and Paul and John. They had never owned a Bible. They knew nothing of the Day of Pentecost or salvation's plan. That meant the door of opportunity stood open wide. At least she wouldn't have to pull them from the mire of spiritual perfidy.

She sang for them. They sat dully with hands folded in numb deadness waiting for the passage of time until they could be served the shortbread. Dorrie cautioned herself not to expect too much too soon. They were like the students in her class who had never held a brush in their hands. They would learn. The first miracle was that they had allowed her a slice of their day for hallowed purposes. Other miracles would follow.

She determined to explain the plan of salvation in its simplicity at the next meeting and to make it a matter of diligent prayer in the meantime. She had two precious and eternal souls dependent upon her ministry.

Inflated expectations slept with her that night. She would tell the salvation story so simply, so beautifully, and with such passion that her grandparents would understand every word and accept it wholeheartedly. She had no doubts.

Next would come Duff. When he was saved, she would no longer have to watch her purse. He would confess his sins and make restitution. She would be delighted to tell him that she had forgiven him long ago, and now Christ had forgiven him, too, just for the asking. He would be her "Billy."

Then Mary would be born into the kingdom, and they would all pray for the return of her husband. Lottie would follow; the chain of events might reach to her "mean man." Goose bumps prickled Dorrie's arms. She hugged the wondrous thoughts. *A missionary!* Who would have thought she would be a missionary?

Yet, in spite of her optimism, the next assembly was even more frustrating. "Do you know that Jesus died for you, Grandfather?" Dorrie asked.

"So my mama told me when I was a kid, but like I told her, I didn't want nor expect anyone to go into that kind of heroics for me. I am big enough to take care of myself."

"Had not Jesus died, Grandfather, you would have no remission of sins. He was buried and rose from the dead the third day to institute a beautiful plan for saving our lost souls." She hurried on. "Those are the three steps to salvation: *We* must crucify *our* flesh, dying out to our sins in repentance. This corresponds with Jesus's death on Calvary. Repentance is telling God we're sorry for every bad thing we have ever done and making a decision not to continue doing those things anymore. Then we are buried in His name in baptism as He was buried, and He will give us the resurrection power of the Holy Ghost. That power will transform us and take us to heaven even as He ascended. We'll know we are born again when we speak in a heavenly language. Oh, it is a wonderful experience! And not only wonderful, it is *necessary*. If the Spirit of Christ dwells in us, He will change our mortal bodies to immortal. . . ." Dorrie had become animated. This was her purpose here, to reveal God's love to her kith and kin who had never known Him.

She paused and looked to them for their responses to the gospel message. Slocum was soundly asleep, and Iantha licked her lips, her eyes glued to the pan of waiting confections that graced the warming oven.

"Can we eat now, Dorrie?" she sighed.

Her grandparents were anchored by the fetters of here and now.

## Chapter 14

# The Suitor

Knight Trotter had chased and had been chased by every eligible maiden in Tulia. His father, the town's leading politician and as devious as his reputation, exercised all the influence of his position to give Knight advantages with the young ladies.

But Dorrie Harris was a different breed. It wasn't only her tawny hair and the golden flecks in her green eyes that gave her appeal. She had a refreshing genuineness that the fake and painted girls he had courted did not possess. She also had a naiveté that might be to his advantage in the future. She would be easily swayed, easily fooled. Knight could not displace her from his mind.

He had a scheme for an unsuspecting girl like Dorrie. Money was his lust, his purpose for existence. Dorrie would be a steppingstone to get him what he wanted.

When he gave her a lift on his recent business trip to Silverton, Knight noticed the glad light flame up in her eyes. That was always a good sign. Given a few more weeks with her power-bitten grandfather, she might be ready to take any road out, to help him accomplish his goal of transferring the old fellow's assets into his own pocket. Then when he had reached this goal—or if the plans developed a glitch—he would simply discard Dorrie as so much worthless baggage. She wasn't his type anyway; she was too religious, too hidebound.

Slocum Dorris might be crotchety, but Knight knew how to handle old codgers. A few gifts, some money under the table, a boodle of promises and pretty, flattering words would turn the worst of them to putty. Yes, that would be the place to start: with Slocum Dorris.

Knight had always pined to get his hands on Mr. Dorris's store. The establishment was turning an obese profit. Linking with Dorrie would serve a dual purpose. . . .

The first platform of Knight's campaign was to hang around the general store polishing Slocum's nose, getting him bridle ready. When Dorrie was there, he leaped at every chance to prove himself a gentleman: opening doors, lifting boxes, running errands. When Dorrie wasn't there, he spent his time in the feed room making points with her grandfather.

"I've been thinking, Mr. Dorris," he remarked rather casually one day. "You have a fetching granddaughter who will be husband hunting before long. You and I both know there isn't an excess of worthy candidates on this prairie."

"She hasn't mentioned marriage."

"Oh, when they're that age, they don't. It's all bottled up inside. They just up and elope when you least expect it. I've seen several of the local bums eyeing her—"

"If one of them touches her, I'll have him arrested!"

"Oh, they wouldn't dare. But my point is that she

might go off with someone willingly. The *wrong* someone. And that could hurt you and your business. To prevent that happening, perhaps I should be the one to rescue her. I have money, and my father has political influence. If I married your granddaughter, we could all work together in this family business and make a fortune. As you know, it takes an ingenious man to keep this store running with enough cover to keep it warm. I am intelligent enough to do it."

Slocum Dorris pulled at his chin. "I don't know—"

"Would you allow me to woo her?"

"Dorrie has a mind of her own. On the minus side, she's a religious fanatic. On the plus side, she's a good cook and an easy keeper. She would never give either of us a fret in this business. She can keep her tongue."

"I tell you what, Mr. Dorris," Knight rubbed his hands together, "just drop a good word for me now and then, and watch me win her over."

At the supper table, Slocum brought Knight's name into the conversation. "He is the nicest chap in this neck of the country, Iantha," he said. "He has money, good looks, and a fine carriage to boot."

Dorrie lowered her eyes to study the tines on her fork. It was the first—and finest—compliment she had ever heard her grandfather give a customer.

"And, Iantha," he continued, "I'm thinking he has an interest in Dorrie. He asked if he might call on her. Would you object to that, Iantha?"

"No," she said, and Dorrie blushed.

"Would you spark him, Dorrie?" Mr. Dorris asked.

"I would have to know that he is a Christian," Dorrie murmured, still inspecting her fork.

"Oh, the very best!" exaggerated her grandfather. "I asked him that question myself, knowing how much it meant to you."

"Maybe he could join us in our Bible studies," she suggested.

"I invited him," Slocum embroidered. "He said that would be impossible since he leads the songs at his own church in Tulia, and they can't spare him. If we could move him over here permanently, though, he could help to lead us all in the right direction. Especially Mary's boys. Duffy thinks Knight hung the moon and stars."

At daylight the next morning, Dorrie set her bread, punching it with flour-whitened hands. Then she left the house for a walk to the windmill. The early hour was worth her sacrifice of comfort; she wanted to be alone to think.

The retrospection included her life with William, Nellie, and Billy. Her thoughts incorporated Grandmother Harris. She supposed they had all forgotten her, evidenced by the many letters she had written and the lack of response to any of them. She had long since run out of postage for further correspondence, but what mattered? She had lost heart for a one-sided communiqué. As for Gabriel Holt, she was nothing to him but a respected teacher who had helped him gain his diploma. Her life and her future were here, and she must use what building blocks she could find to create a livable world for herself.

Could Knight be a part of it? Her grandfather liked him. Duff liked him. Could she be happy with Knight? She wasn't sure. Just now her feelings seemed independent of intelligent reason. Nevertheless, if he could meld the Dorris family together in spirit and unity, would it not be worth the price of her heart to see her family salvaged? Yes, it would be worth it! She would do her best to love the man.

On the way back to the house, Dorrie saw Iantha digging behind the barn again. Poor darling! Grief had driven her to unearth her son's picture once more. A new thought commuted with Dorrie's sympathy. If Iantha wished, she could paint a large portrait from the small photo. It would make a lovely holiday gift.

Dorrie gave the barn a wide berth so as not to disturb her sorrowing grandmother. There would be another headache. . . .

That evening, Knight came as a guest to supper. He raved over the dumplings and corn fritters made by Dorrie. "With a cook like this one, we might go into the restaurant business and become millionaires, Mr. Dorris," he jested, giving Dorrie a conspiratorial wink.

"Didn't I tell you that Dorrie is no slouch for a cook? Wait until you taste the bread pudding."

Iantha had been ill all day, and she excused herself to her room. Slocum took the wing-backed chair but soon fell asleep. That left Knight and Dorrie to entertain themselves; it was the first of many such evenings. Dorrie began to look forward to these times of fun and fellowship.

When Duff attended, the boy giggled like a girl at Knight's lighthearted puns, providing Knight an audience for his clowning. With his wit and drollery, he succeeded in taking Dorrie's mind from more serious matters, and the way he handled Slocum and Iantha was nothing short of a marvel.

Knight's familiarity—the winks, the pats, and the

endearing names—were as much a part of his personality as his blue eyes were contributors to his good looks. He called Dorrie "baby doll" and "honey" until she grew accustomed to his affectionate demeanor and liked it.

One evening, Knight asked Mr. Dorris if he might sit with Dorrie alone. Slocum nodded, almost as if the idea had been preplanned, and took himself to bed. To loosen the atmosphere, Knight amused Dorrie by rehearsing antics of his childhood. These stories were chock-full of humor, and if his design was to put her at ease, it worked. She was beginning to feel that she could enjoy this man's company for a lifetime. The depth of emotion she had felt when she'd looked into Gabe's eyes was not there yet. But it would come.

The hour grew later, and still they chatted, forgetting the clock. Knight's question entered unexpectedly. "Have you ever considered marriage, Dorrie? You're such a brilliant girl and so very pretty. You must not waste your life in servitude to two old people."

Dorrie's face burned. "Oh, I'm not *wasting* it, Knight. I am trying to lead my grandparents to salvation. God sent me here. I owe it to them to—"

Without warning, he placed his hand on hers, and she made no effort to remove it. "I've always wanted a wife who could make bread pudding. Now I think I have found her. Would you consider being my cook?"

"I will pray about it."

"Pray? Pray tell, why pray?"

"I pray about everything."

"But about *marriage*? Why? Marriage is *ordained* of God, and some decisions He leaves up to us. Does He tell you what you should fix for supper or what dress you should wear tomorrow? He expects us to use our own brains for some things, sweetheart."

"God knows things that I don't know."

"I fail to understand why God would care whether you cook bread pudding for me or for someone else," he snapped. She wasn't proving to be the pushover he had hoped. "It's your choice and mine!"

"God will help me to know." Dorrie pulled her hand away from him. "I can't tell you how I will know, but I will."

"When will you know?"

"God will not keep us waiting long." She gave him a disarming smile.

It was past midnight when Dorrie knelt beside her bed, the impression of Knight's kiss lingering on her cheek. Marrying Knight could be the perfect solution to *everything*. Everyone would be pleased, even Mary and Lottie. She would have the leisure to paint again. . . .

Dorrie burrowed beneath her sheet, dizzy with Knight's proposal. A rich and handsome man had asked her to marry him. They would live happily ever after. This was fairy tale fabric!

The night held her in folds of uneasy sleep. She tossed and turned. Something was wrong. What could it be? The answer stepped almost within her reach; then it eluded her.

## Chapter 15

# Arrest

*I will be occupied in Tulia for a few days*, Knight's note said. His father had been called out of town, he explained, and he was left to man the hotel. He would miss Dorrie dreadfully and would count the hours until they could be together again. They would make their wedding plans when he returned to Tule Canyon.

Dorrie missed him, too, but his absence gave her an opportunity to seek the will of God in the matter. Marriage was a commitment for life. When Knight was there, he colored her thinking with his sanguine outlook on everything, and it worried her.

Although Knight Trotter laid claim to a walk with the Master, Dorrie found herself wondering. When the conversation turned to biblical truths, he took the verbal reins and steered the discussion another direction. The transaction wasn't overt; it was subtle, almost unnoticeable. When she asked if he had been born again, he said that he was born there in Swisher County. Then when he perceived that her connotation was spiritual, he explained that the term "born again" wasn't frequently used in their part of the country, but yes, he had experienced that transformation. He couldn't recall his exact age when he was baptized.

Slocum asked if Dorrie could work an extra shift at the store that week. Business in the feed store had increased; everyone wanted to stock up on feed for the winter. Dorrie welcomed the diversion. Without Knight, the hours dragged.

On Wednesday, Duff was sick, and with Knight out too, they ran shorthanded on help. Slocum needed Dorrie to deliver a jar of pickling vinegar to a Mrs. Jule, whose house clung to the hem of Silverton. Duff usually made this particular delivery. The lady wanted to make some chow chow, he said, and needed the ingredient right away. He would pay Dorrie extra, he promised. He cautioned her to go directly to the address he had given her and come back immediately. Time was of the essence today.

Dorrie was glad to make the call; the walk would do her good. If she were to be married, the extra money would come in handy as well. She took the sack that Slocum gave her and started for town. Her mind was on Knight—her knight in shining armor—whom she had decided to wed. As Knight had said, the decision was hers; God would not make it for her. She couldn't live on memories of Gabriel. Yesterday's wind could not turn today's windmill.

The sandy road was deserted until she neared the village, where she met a man on horseback. She moved off the road to let him pass. He tipped his hat and rode on.

A piece of paper caught beneath a rock arrested her

attention. Some sixth sense compelled her to stoop and pick it up. A chill gripped her, sending a deepening coldness to the center of her being and freezing her spirit. It was one of the letters to Nellie. The stamp had been removed; it had never been mailed.

Farther on, she saw another envelope. Then another. And another. Nellie hadn't received a single letter. Duff had purposely mislaid them. Her mother didn't even know where she was. She must be beside herself with worry!

Engulfed in the depravity of her situation, Dorrie stood bewildered and obsessed by a racking agony. What could she do? She must get word to the Harrises at once. As soon as she delivered the vinegar, she would go directly to the postal office and dispatch a letter to Nellie. She would be disobeying her grandfather's orders for an expeditious return, but surely he would understand. How needlessly her mother must have suffered! A sob caught on a lump in Dorrie's throat.

She considered whether to go straight to the post office and then deliver the flask on her way back to Tule Canyon or to make the grocery stop first, but the jar was growing heavy. She could make better time if she rid herself of its weight.

Finding the correct house was no problem; Slocum had given careful and explicit directions so there would be no doubts as to her destination. Mrs. Jule opened the door and grabbed the sack. The woman pulled it inside quickly, hardly taking time for a civil greeting. "Mr. Jule will pay tomorrow," she clipped her words and closed the door.

The sawed-off contact didn't bother Dorrie. She was frantic to get on about the business of letting her mother know her whereabouts. Her mind left Mrs. Jule and her rudeness with her first step away from the woman's house.

The sound of a horse's hooves brought her head up. The rider, a large man in uniform, rode toward her. She tried to step out of his way. "Halt, miss," he ordered, "and don't move." He strode to the house she had just left and demanded the parcel Dorrie had delivered.

Opening the jar, he put his nose to it. "Just as I thought," he said, stern rebuke on his swarthy face. "Liquor."

"But, sir," Mrs. Jule objected, "I made a *grocery* order. I had no idea what was in the package. The girl—"

"Yes, come with me, miss," he commanded. "You are under arrest for possession of and transporting an unlawful substance. I am Silverton's constable, Bill Briggs." He spoke with the haughtiness of one whose authority had gone to his head. "You have broken the prohibition laws of our county, and you will stand trial for it."

"Sir, I was only making a delivery for my grandfather—"

"That's what they all say, girlie. We've been trying to break this bootlegging ring for months now. I got my big tip today. At last we're making progress."

"But you can ask my grandfather. Mrs. Jule needed the pickling vinegar to make chow chow from her green tomatoes, and—"

The constable hooted. "Now I've heard it all! Pickling vinegar, my eye! It might be pickled corn squeezings. I know whiskey when I smell it."

Dorrie backed away, trying to pull her wrist from his firm grasp.

"Don't resist arrest, miss," he admonished. "That will constitute yet another infraction of the law, and you have enough charges as it is." His attitude was devoid of compassion or interest in her future.

Dorrie stood ridge-pole straight. "I demand that you take me to my grandfather, Slocum Dorris."

"We'll bring him in, all right. But you'll go with me now."

"Wh—where?"

"To the jail." He hoisted her onto the horse as if she were a rag doll and led the horse away.

Everyone on Main Street paused to gape at her as she went by. Storekeepers came to their front entrances to gawk. Mothers shooed their children behind their skirts, and little boys pointed. One freckled-faced urchin waved, lending friendliness to curiosity. The taste of shame filled Dorrie's mouth. How could a law officer make such a flagrant mistake? He would pay for this when Knight Trotter got a hold of him! Knight would make him apologize to the entire community.

"I need to stop and post a letter, please," Dorrie requested.

"Perhaps you fail to understand, miss, that your rights ended when you committed a crime," the constable said in an inflexible voice.

Dorrie dug around in her conscience and unearthed nothing. They would realize their error, ask her a few questions, and send her home, of course. How mortified her grandparents would be when they learned that their granddaughter had been mistakenly arrested! And, oh, Nellie would *die*!

At the city hall, she was seated on a hard bench. She

didn't like the smell of the place: stale cigar smoke, unemptied spittoons, and aging paint. The single window was so filthy that everything on the other side of it lost definition. A bunched square of green carpet lay on the floor.

A man entered with a tablet to transcribe what Dorrie said. "Your name, miss?"

"Susan Dorris Harris."

"Harris being your married name?"

"No, sir. I'm not married. Harris is the name of my adoptive parents."

"Have you relatives in this vicinity?"

"Yes, sir. Slocum and Iantha Dorris of Tule Canyon are my grandparents."

"Your birth parents' names?"

"Both of them are deceased, sir."

"Your occupation?"

"I am an art teacher."

The man hacked a harsh, dry laugh. "Your age?"

"I turned twenty-one last week."

"Good. You're of legal age to be tried as an adult."

"Tried for what, sir?"

"Playing ignorant will get you nowhere, ma'am. Will you have legal counsel?"

"My grandfather will clear up this misunderstanding."

"I hope so. Good day, ma'am."

"May I go now?"

"Yes, you will go now." They took her purse and her umbrella. "To your cell."

## Chapter 16

# Abandoned

Dorrie felt, as well as heard, the cold, metallic clang of finality when the jailer closed and locked the cubicle with his large, flat key.

She had never been inside a jail. It was dark and dismal, a spirit-dampening place located behind the city hall. There were six cells, three on one side of a narrow walkway and three on the other. Expensive, modern locks guarded the barred doors.

"When will my grandfather be here to take me home?" she asked, speaking desperately to the man's retreating back.

He whirled about. "He will be notified tomorrow. The wheels of justice turn slowly, but they are sure." He walked out.

Dorrie dropped onto the rigid slab that would serve as her chair, her bed, and her table. She stared at the gray stone walls, her dignity offended. Well, she would only have to spend one measly night here. What was one night out of a lifetime? She would be tough and show her *Harris* courage.

Knight would find it ludicrous; he made a joke of everything. He might be angry with the constable, but he would be proud of her. This would be one occasion where she'd welcome the purgative of his comedy. She longed to see him, to talk with him.

The jailer brought her a thin fish soup for her supper. It reminded her of dirty dishwater. When she found a fly in the evil-smelling broth, she set it aside untouched; she could afford to miss one meal. But when the jailer returned, he scolded her. "Best you eat every scrap they send you, lady. They don't offer big helpings or seconds. You don't want to get sick and die in here."

"I'll be out tomorrow anyhow," she quipped, a bit smugly.

There was nothing to do with this idle time. She wished for her sketchbook, her Bible, or a writing tablet. Every hour spanned an individual eon. Why couldn't they contact her grandfather today? They *wanted* her to be punished—and for something she was not guilty of. Oh, well, when she didn't show up at the store within a reasonable length of time, her grandfather would come looking for her. He would find her, rescue her.

She beguiled herself by painting mental pictures. She would marry Knight, and someday he would take her back to Cleburne, where she would introduce him to Nellie and William. "He's *terribly* handsome, Dorrie," Nellie would say. If Duff—contrary Duff—liked Knight, then surely Billy would. Knight would tell Billy about his infamous sister who spent a night imprisoned. He would call her Belle Starr, the notorious lady outlaw, and they would all laugh. Would Grandmother Harris be pleased with her marriage to Knight? A burr of doubt pricked Dorrie's mind. Grandmother Harris would say that Knight wasn't her type. Martha would consider Knight shallow, unspiritual.

The evening darkened into night, consigning Dorrie to a pit of inky blackness. She quoted every passage of Scripture she could remember to allay her disquietude then curled up on the abrasive bench, pulling her feet beneath her skirts. She refused her mind the license to retrace the harsh, bitter day. It would soon be over, and distantly viewed, it would be less atrocious, maybe even humorous. At least, she could be grateful that the temperature was pleasant. It was neither too hot nor too cold.

Settling herself as best she could for what she supposed would be a miserable night, Dorrie fell into a sound sleep in five minutes. The emotional turmoil had taken its toll on her body.

The shuffling of feet, the clinking of an iron door, and the screech of a woman awakened her, bringing craven fear. She didn't know where she was, only that she didn't like being there. She seemed to be in a shadowed cave. Was she a victim of some demonic nightmare? She bolted to her feet in time to see the jailer pushing and pulling a small woman toward the ward across from her. The irate woman, who wore a black felt hat, high heeled shoes, big pearl earrings, and silk stockings, spewed oaths, flailing, biting, and kicking in every direction at once.

"What—what is the matter?" asked Dorrie.

"She's drunk, miss."

When the woman turned toward her, Dorrie saw that it was Mrs. Jule, the customer who had ordered the vinegar.

"I'm here because of *you*," she screamed, jabbing a long-boned finger at Dorrie. Anointing her with profanity, she yelled, "It is *your* fault."

"Sir, I really must speak to my grandfather at once," Dorrie told the jailer, her agitation apparent.

"That is the constable's responsibility, not mine," said the jailer.

Breakfast arrived, a piece of dry bread and a cup of lukewarm milk ready to sour. Dorrie choked it down and hoped it would stay. Surely someone would come to have her released before noon.

Hours followed other endless hours. Mrs. Jule's husband appeared to pay her fine and to take her home. "See you next week, Mrs. Jule," the jailer said with a hint of sarcasm.

Time lost clarity; Dorrie's only timetable was the meals, if they could be called that, served with strict punctuality. The noon fare was a saltless cabbage stew. Dorrie longed for a bath and a change of clothes. What was keeping her grandfather?

The supper hour came with the worst food yet, and Dorrie began to feel frantic. Surely she wouldn't have to spend another night in this wretched place! She asked the jailer for an explanation of the delay, but he only shrugged. She hoped that Knight would report the uncooperative man to the proper authorities and have him dismissed.

By the third day, Dorrie was near tears. Even the Harris courage was wearing thin. This punishment had gone on long enough! She was inventing a few threats silently when the constable stopped in to talk with her. "We have contacted Mr. Slocum Dorris, whom you claim as your grandfather, and he professes no knowledge of you whatsoever, Miss Harris. He tells us that he has no granddaughter and that you are lying."

"Then send for Knight Trotter," she demanded, on the edge of hysteria. "He will have me released."

"The son of Mr. Trotter, the politician?"

"Yes."

"We will get word to him, Miss Harris. However, it may take a couple of days. Tulia is twenty miles away." The constable left.

*A couple of days!* She was weeping, but it didn't matter. There was no one to hear, and it was a relief to give vent to her misery and let it all pour out.

Why had her grandfather disowned her? Did he believe that she committed some shameful crime? Couldn't he have come to hear her side of the story? Didn't he understand that sometimes even law enforcement officers made mistakes? What about her grandmother?

Regardless, Knight was a bedrock she could count on. The constable would rue the day he arrested her when she rode away in Knight's grand carriage. She hated that she would be rumpled and begrimed when Knight came for her. She hadn't even a brush to care for her tresses. But a love like Knight's would overlook trivialities.

Hope and the eagerness to see her fiancé again buoyed her through the next two days of scant nourishment and poor hygiene. Finding a restful position became more and more difficult as her bones protested louder and louder against the brutality of the unyielding bunk. She grew stiff and sore and longed for the luxury of a pillow beneath her head.

Knight. She hoped that when Knight came they might be married right away. The disappointment she had suffered through her grandfather's abandonment would not be easily reconciled in her mind. She had given much and received little in return. She would insist that she and Knight move to Tulia, where they could live in serene independence. Slocum said that Knight led the singing at his church; she would be glad to play the piano for his accompaniment. Oh, to attend a worship service again!

The constable finally returned as he had promised. The sight of him was a fallacious encouragement. "I'm dreadfully sorry, Miss Harris," he said. "One of my deputies contacted Mr. Knight Trotter, and he said that he had only met you on one occasion when you came through Tulia. He said that he can take no responsibility for your unlawful actions. I'm afraid you will have to bear the consequences of your crime to the fullest extent of the law."

Dorrie dropped her head in a slow, final acceptance of fate. She was in a deep well of pain, drawn irrevocably from those she had supposed cared for her. None of them believed she was innocent, not even Knight. There was no one for her. No one. The hurt and stunned bitterness that she experienced brought such an oppression to her heart that it hampered her breathing and robbed her of every vestige of strength. She had a horrible sense of spiraling downward ever swifter into a fearful vortex.

All that night, all the next day, and through the next night, time forced upon her the ruthless certainty that she was friendless. The last of her illusions died. She paced the floor of her cell, contemplating her appalling predicament. No one could help her but God.

## Chapter 17

# Illness

For a few forlorn hours, Dorrie's spirit strove to go on in a magnificent reproof of those who had betrayed her, especially Knight. Endless, futile questions raged in her heart. But like the trunk of a tree cut deep into its heart, she began to weaken and wither within, her string of hope fraying into a useless tangle of despair. Her physical strength failed, and it seemed that many years passed. The parson, a man whose lean frame reproved waste and excess, made his monthly visit to the jail. He was accustomed to cursing, belligerent men who railed against God and society, but the sight of a young woman locked away, and a lovely one at that, wrenched his heart. Women were soft and delicate; prison was no place for the fairest of God's creatures.

The girl's eyes reminded him of a cornered animal, frightened and desperate. He didn't know what her charges were, but he decided to send his good wife to pay her a call at once. However, when Celia Boston visited the jail, she did not recognize the disheveled Dorrie as the girl who had visited her a few weeks earlier. Dorrie was too embarrassed by her confinement to make herself known to the only friend she had on the high plains of Texas. Celia's one-sided conversation dwindled and then died. There was nothing to say and no reason to say it. When Celia offered to say a prayer for Dorrie's "wayward soul," Dorrie thanked her, offering no self-defense.

Thereafter, Dorrie's food sat on the dirty floor uneaten. Her body, ignited with a scorching fire, spurned it. Thick, strange lights appeared and vanished while dull sounds rushed in from somewhere, filling all. Distant voices drifted from outside her cell, but whether they were real or imagined she could not tell. Neither could she determine whether or not their subject should have any significance to her.

"I'm not sure, Bill, that we are any nearer to breaking the bootlegging ring than we were," the county sheriff pondered. "This girl was the cat's paw, and her arrest has only driven the real culprits deeper into hiding. The core of this fester is the bootleggers themselves."

"Yes, sheriff, we *are* gaining ground. We've learned much from this girl's capture. At least, we know now who the moonshiners are *not*."

"What do you mean by that?"

"It was rumored that Mr. Dorris's old store was a dispensary for the grog and that the old man himself might be a distiller and an agent. Now we know that can't be true because it was Slocum Dorris's own grandson who tipped me off about this girl."

"The boy called Duff?"

"None other. So you see, they are working for us and not against us."

"Not necessarily, Bill. They could have set the girl up, used her as a smoke screen. I still contend that someone employed the girl for their devious purposes then left her to suffer the consequences alone, consequences they should be sharing."

"She broke the law, sheriff, and we cannot wink at crime," argued Silverton's peace officer. "This town must know that I mean business. I will not tolerate lawlessness in man, woman, boy, or girl. If villainy is what you want in your county, I will step down and move out of town. But I warn you, you will have a heap of trouble on your hands. Children will no longer be safe on our streets—"

"But isn't this a first offense for the young woman? You have not been able to discover a previous criminal record of any kind. Why can't we just impose a stiff fine and let her go? I dare say she has learned her lesson well. It doesn't take much to scare a woman into right living. In fact, I would be most interested to see where she would go from here."

"She has been abandoned. Someone deposited her trunk and all her belongings on the steps of the city hall. They came during the night."

"The yellow cowards! Wouldn't it be nice if we could identify people by the fingerprints they leave behind?"

"It would indeed."

"The girl has no relatives?"

"None that we can find. She made the ridiculous claim that Mr. Dorris, who runs that country store, is her grandfather. He hooted at the idea!

"And listen to this: she even claimed that the politician Trotter's son was her boyfriend. We looked him up, and he laughed at her foolish fiction. He said he had never laid eyes on her but once and that was when he transported her here from Tulia. He runs a taxi service of sorts, you know, with his father's fancy rig. He said he deposited her at Slocum Dorris's store, and that was the last he saw of her. He thought she was just wandering around the country looking for trouble. We checked with the postal office, and no mail has ever been sent there for her. None of her stories can hold water."

"Is she—mentally unbalanced?"

"Oh, no. She is quite sane."

"And she has no money?"

"There is some small change in her purse." He smirked. "Women of her caliber can come up with money, officer."

The sheriff lifted an eyebrow. "Your city could probably use the funds right now. I say, give her a stiff fine and let her go."

"You are welcome to interview her yourself and make a recommendation to the judge, sir. I did my duty when I made the arrest in keeping with my election promises."

A metal door scraped open, but Dorrie didn't move. She didn't even attempt to sit up; her head felt too heavy to lift.

"Miss Harris?"

Dorrie moistened her burning lips. From the eerie, muffling fog, she tried to answer, but no words came. They stuck in the deadness of her throat. She felt wretched and sick and unutterably old.

"I believe the girl is ill, Bill," pointed out the sheriff, alarmed. "Her skin is flushed."

"She's a con artist, sheriff," sniffed the constable. "This kind can play dead to get what she wants. And what she wants is out of here."

The sheriff placed a hand on Dorrie's forehead. "She is feverish," he announced, "and it won't be good publicity for you if a female dies in your jail. Public opinion is a fickle thing. This case could turn and rend you. Women are still sacred items to many Westerners, you know. It matters not what she has done; the townsfolk will forget that as the dirt falls on her casket. *You'll* be the bad guy. It'll be *your* funeral. You had better get her to Amarillo to the hospital and worry about the sentencing or her fine later—if she survives."

The sheriff's alarm pinched Bill Briggs. "Who could take her?"

"Have you a parson here in Silverton?"

"Parson Boston."

"He would likely do it. Charity is his department."

"How soon—?"

"The sooner, the better. You'd best get her away from Silverton. You can't afford to have her dying here!"

## Chapter 18

# The Transfer

"This girl is very ill, Harold," Celia Boston said to her husband. "My medical training tells me that only prayer will keep her soul and body together until we reach the infirmary. Please help me pray."

"I'm praying, Celia."

"Can't you go faster?"

"I'm going as fast as the buggy will travel. The wheels are in danger of catching fire at the speed we're traveling now."

"We need angels around us."

"We have them."

"What did you say the girl's name is?"

"Susan Harris."

"A young lady by the name of Harris paid me a visit a few weeks ago. She promised to attend church but didn't show up. Her name wasn't Susan, though, and she was a schoolteacher. She was a wonderful Christian; I had hoped she would provide us some music. I wonder—"

"Do you suppose, Celia, that this girl could be a sister to the one who called on you? Sometimes sisters take very different roads in life."

"That is a possibility. Did you learn what put this girl behind bars?"

"She became involved with an illegal operation of making and selling whiskey."

Celia shuddered. "And so young."

"Sin is a terrible taskmaster."

"For such Christ died, Harold."

"Yes, dear. It behooves us to hate the sin and love the sinner. That's His way."

Dorrie knew nothing of the Bostons' deliberations. She was oblivious to her surroundings, feeling nothing, hearing nothing, seeing nothing. A merciful state of unconsciousness enveloped her, aided and abetted by her loss of heart and lack of nourishment. She existed in a dreamlike era where there was no light, no sound, and no movement.

"What shall we do with her—with her corpse if she dies?" Celia asked.

"That is not faith, wife. We will take one moment at a time."

Much to Celia's surprise, Dorrie was yet alive when they reached Amarillo. However, the doctor's prognosis did nothing to encourage her. "I have little hope for this girl," he said, "but we will try as best we can to save her life."

Pastor Boston thanked him, and he and Celia headed for Silverton, glad they weren't carrying funereal news to the mayor. It would be safe to say they prayed most of the way home.

## EIGHTEEN / THE TRANSFER

A long interval of darkness claimed Dorrie, leaving her slack and empty. She lay in a cave of apathy, tortured by horrors that were not physical. Death would be an advantageous end to her ordeal. But the flicker of life in one's youth cannot be easily extinguished. The spirit fights on after the body has given up.

On the seventh day of Dorrie's hospitalization, the fever lost its deathly grip, relinquishing its hold on her spent and shrunken frame. The faint, faraway voices that moved over her became more distinct; they edged in closer. Everyone was dressed in white. Was she in heaven?

"Where . . . where am I?" she whispered to a face that blurred in space.

"You're in the hospital, Miss Harris," an intern answered. "We thought we were going to lose you."

"Lose me?"

"You have been seriously ill."

"Oh. How did I get here?"

"The parson from Silverton and his wife brought you here."

"From Silverton?"

Memory seeped back, and Dorrie's emotions slowly roused, emotions that had been numbed by the long, menacing hours in the jail where she had sat awaiting the bursting storm of injustice. Had the constable realized his error and released her?

"How long will I be here?"

"For a while yet."

"Will I be sent—back—when I'm well?" Terror filled her eyes along with a puddle of tears. "I don't want to go—back. I'd rather die!"

"The doctor has been in contact with the authorities

of your county. He is trying to work out a plan whereby you may pay your fine and be free when you leave here."

"My fine?"

"You may be able to offer money for the dismissal of the charges that are against you."

"But, sir, I am guilty of no crime."

"That may be so, miss. But since you have no advocate, it might be better to quietly pay the fee and put it all behind you. That wouldn't be admitting to guilt; it would simply be the fastest way out of an inequitable situation."

"I—I cannot pay, sir. I have no money."

"Please rest, Miss Harris, and worry about that later. God takes care of His children."

Dorrie gave her attendant a faded smile. "Ah, there," he coaxed. "One smile before noon is worth two after."

With convalescence came restlessness. Dorrie's hands longed to hold a paintbrush or a ball of bread dough or a needle. She craved beauty and color. With maddening persistence, her mind traveled back to her girlhood home. To the bluebonnets and larkspur and buttercups. To her family. How foolish she had been to leave William and Nellie and Billy, walking away from love and security! She didn't doubt that they would take her back unequivocally, but she shrank from letting them know where she was and under what circumstances. She could not bring a blotch to the good Harris name.

How far she had fallen! She'd had a good job, an unimpeachable heritage with her adoptive family, a budding friendship with Gabriel Holt that might have been nurtured into a full-blown romance, and a worshipful half-brother. What more could a young woman have wanted? She had given it all up for what? A grandfather who disowned her? A thieving, disrespectful cousin? A prospective bridegroom who dropped her when she was apprehended for a crime she did not commit? What a ridiculous barter she had made! Oh, if she could call back time! With her hard-earned wisdom, she would forget her foolish quest and take the best.

The nurse came in with a pot of wilted flowers. "One of the patients who left the hospital this morning asked me to give these to someone who needed them," she said. "I thought of you."

"Thank you. They are beautiful."

"They are a bit droopy, but we'll nurse them back to health."

The splash of color was a welcome escape from the bleak stone walls in which Dorrie existed. She loved flowers. "And we have your personal belongings here. They were sent up from Silverton. Is there anything you'd like from your grip?"

In a final edict of rejection, her grandparents had thrown her out, clothes and all. "Is my sketchbook there?" Dorrie asked.

The nurse found the tablet, and Dorrie's hands shook as she reached for it. It had been a lifetime since she had painted. It was almost as if the work portrayed in the notebook—sketches tinted with mild washes of watercolor—was not her own.

She studied each small drawing with an analyst's scrutiny. There was the old adobe shack she had captured in Seminole. It stood in lilac against the purple shadows lengthened by the setting sun. The windmill scene brought attention to the water in its reservoir as blue as hyacinths. In the foreground, yellow sunflowers followed the sun with their faces. She had painted a canyon wall that resembled a row of books with pages partly opened. Finally, there was a picture of the chaotic wilderness, its scattered rocks carved and broken into every conceivable shape. Some people kept diaries; she painted to preserve her memories.

The rest of the pages were blank. She'd had neither the desire nor the leisure for her artwork in Tule Canyon. She had been too busy in the creative effort of keeping Iantha Dorris's littered home from becoming a pig's sty.

Unnoticed, the nurse stood beside her. "What lovely pictures!" she exclaimed, bringing Dorrie back from a remote region. "Where did you get them?"

"I—I painted them."

"*You* painted them? *Yourself?*"

"Yes."

"Why, you are a professional, Miss Harris! Those pictures are worthy of a gallery! How long have you been painting?"

"Most of my life. I was an art teacher before—before—" The sentence broke in the middle.

"Why, you could sell your work! Do you do portraits—of people, I mean?"

"Yes, ma'am. I enjoy painting people. The last portrait I painted was of my Grandmother Harris. It turned out well."

"You have a grandmother?"

Dorrie realized too late that she had revealed too much, had given information she had not intended. "That was—some time ago." She looked away to hide the wound in her soul that had not healed and never would. To speak of Martha Harris made it bleed anew.

The nurse led her away from the anguish. "There is a child here, a patient of our hospital, who cannot live for long. Her mother has no picture to remember her by. Would you paint one for her?"

"I would be glad to!" The request gave Dorrie a reason for existence, provided an antidote for the bitterness of her imponderable fate. A better plan could not have been devised to forward Dorrie's recovery.

Dorrie poured her heart, as well as her talent, into the project. The child was like a beautiful nymph even amid her frequent paroxysms of convulsions. Dorrie fashioned a perfect replica of the little head with its tousled, bright curls and its small, oval face possessed of dark eyes, strangely luminous.

The gratitude the mother heaped upon Dorrie gave her real joy, her first feeling of worth since the constable gripped her arm at Mrs. Jule's house. With this true work of art, Dorrie experienced a new and exquisite birth of character. Whatever the future, she now knew herself. She knew who she was: her strengths, her weaknesses, and her reasons for existence. One's natural genealogy counted for little. God, in His infinite wisdom, had placed her where she could develop to her greatest potential.

Her mind was settled. She would pray her way through her present maze, and when she was clear, she would return to the home that God had given her—her family, her people, not by virtue of birth but by divine appointment. This trial would be a steppingstone rather than a headstone for her hopes and dreams.

Outside, the entire west burgeoned in one magnificent blaze of glory.

## CHAPTER 19

# Assignment

The doctor sat behind his cluttered desk, facing Dorrie. "You are well enough for dismissal, Miss Harris," he stated, "but I fear that if I send you back into confinement, you will have a relapse. We scarcely pulled you through this time; next time we might not be so fortunate. The authorities are willing to settle with you for a substantial fine—"

"How much, sir?"

"Forty dollars."

Dorrie's hands fell like dying things to her side. "I have no money, doctor."

"The nurse tells me you are an exceptional artist. Would you be willing to earn the funds to obtain your freedom by painting?"

"Oh, yes, sir! But it would take a long time to earn that much. And—and where would I stay?"

"You will take residence with those for whom you work. However, wherever you are employed, you will be guarded to some degree to prevent your escape. You must remember that until the fine is paid, you are still a prisoner."

"My escape?"

"You might try to run away."

"Oh, no, sir. I wouldn't do that. I wouldn't wish to spend the rest of my life looking over my shoulder in fright of discovery even though I am guiltless of the charges against me. I want my record purged, and I am the only one to expunge it. Those who could have spoken in my defense have—turned their backs on me." She gave a sudden, elfin smile. "Where would I find a guard who wished his picture painted?"

"There is a wealthy gentleman who has a ranch on the Canadian River and to whom our hospital is indebted." He pointed to a brass plaque above the door that read: *In Honor of Thaddeus Bronsworth.* "His name is Thaddeus Bronsworth, and he built this hospital with his own funds. Now and then he posts a notice in the newspaper for an artist to paint his picture.

"They say he pays well, but I don't mean to imply that your job would be easy. It is also reported that he has never found an artist who can please him. He's a hermit, and he is finicky. I have never seen the man nor has anyone else who works here. He doesn't like people, and all his business transactions are handled by his foreman. He hasn't stepped foot off his land in years."

"Likely, I wouldn't be able to please him, either, sir, and I would have wasted my time."

"Oh, your time wouldn't be wasted. When Mr. Bronsworth dismisses an artist, he pays them for the hours they have spent in the effort. Rumor has it that several artists have quit or refused to accept the job in the first place. Once they have met him, they don't even stay to unpack. I'm sure it would be a challenge, but it would be preferable to returning to Silverton, wouldn't it?"

"Oh, yes! Anything would be better than going—back."

"I could contact Mr. Bronsworth's foreman—"

"I taught my art students that their abilities could only expand by overcoming obstacles. I may have to eat my words. I will admit, though, the more you tell me, the more intrigued I am by the challenge and the more I would like to add my name to this man's roster of artists, whether I succeed or fail. Who knows? I might be the one to please him. What have I to lose?"

"I'd say you have nothing to lose, Miss Harris, and a lot to gain. The man lives several miles from here. You would have to stay on site until you complete your project."

"And be guarded by his foreman?" Her eyes held humor.

"Or the old recluse himself. Then when you are finished, you will return here, and I will be your mediator with the county. Is that agreeable?"

"Quite, sir."

"If Mr. Bronsworth wishes your services, he will send his foreman for you."

A week later, a car arrived to take Dorrie to her assignment. It was a growling, thundering apparatus made by the Ford Company. It was hard to tell whether the operator was prouder of the vehicle or his ability to maneuver it down the street.

The driver was a thickset, middle-aged man whose

skin had been rusted by wind and dust. He bounded from the flivver, bending as far as his paunchy torso would allow. In his greeting was all the archaic grandeur, all the hauteur of an aristocrat. "Miss Harris," he said, "my name is Driver. Leastwise, that's my alias. It will be my pleasure to escort you to the ranch of Thaddeus Bronsworth, Esquire. You will be made content there, I am sure. My employer is a very kind and generous man." So saying, he gathered Dorrie's luggage, stowed it in the rumble seat of the coupe, and helped her in.

His evaluation of Mr. Bronsworth, Dorrie mused, was the opposite of all other versions. The accounts were so diverse, in fact, as to puzzle her. But who would know a man better than his foreman? She was eager to meet the controversial magnate for herself.

The ride was a pleasant one, accomplished under clear skies and a lazy breeze. Their route took them through a terrain of Spartan beauty. The road curved and looped by rolling hills, sandstone plateaus, and bear grass just turning a mellow shade of yellow. Dorrie wished she could stop long enough to paint a landscape scene for Nellie's enjoyment.

The nearer they got to the ranch, the more Dorrie recognized the dominion of a river. Large cottonwood trees broke the monotony of the land with their sheathed bark, dead snags, and dry, sweet odor. At one point, the road swung so closely to the river that Dorrie could hear the gurgling of water.

Presently, they turned onto a private road that disappeared into a swale of salt cedars. "We are on Thad's ranch now," Driver said. "A parcel of ground, people claim, that does not readily give up its secrets." He chuckled.

They came to a gate, which Driver opened with a long key. The gate had iron bars set closely. Obviously, people were not meant to get in unannounced. Stone monuments that flanked the entrance bore the initials T. B. After driving the car through, Driver closed the gate behind them; it locked with a spring. *I probably won't need a guard*, thought Dorrie wryly. *I'm locked in again, only my cell is much larger this time.*

The foursquare ranch house, its windows blinking reflected sunlight, sat on a gradually rising bench of land. It was a squatty, many-roomed edifice made of stone and boasting a covered porch that ran its full width. "This is Bronsworth Estates, ma'am," the driver made his valiant attempt at bowing again with as little results as before. "I am at your service at all times and will go to any extreme to see that your stay here is an unforgettable one, which I am sure it will be. If you have a need, lay it upon me." He rang the bell, and a woman appeared, a hurrying, bustling little woman with a face-splitting smile.

"Miss Harris!" she babbled. "I've been waiting dinner for you. How refreshing it will be to have another woman around the house. Most of the artists have been men."

"You are Mrs. Bronsworth?"

"Oh, no, no!" She laid her hand across her mouth to stop her gleeful laughter. "I'm the cook and housekeeper for Mr. Bronsworth. He isn't married. But you shall meet him for yourself, and—well, maybe that will explain things." She changed the subject. "I will show you to your room, and you can freshen up before our evening meal. From henceforth, breakfast will be at eight, lunch at one, and dinner at six. Is that agreeable?"

"Whatever your schedule is will suit me, Mrs.—?"

"Wilda. Call me Wilda." She led Dorrie through an open courtyard built in the house's center. Her shoes pounded a rhythm on the terrazzo floor.

Dorrie's room was large and airy, its walls papered with a dainty flowered pattern. The bed, spread with a luxurious comforter the color of wet plums, had high posters the hue of honey and as smooth as satin. Intricate carvings of birds and flowers garnished the headboard. Feeling like a weary desert traveler who had stumbled onto an oasis, Dorrie breathed a sigh. "This is gorgeous!"

"And you will have your own bath," the housekeeper added. "Mr. Bronsworth is ingenious. He has installed a complete plumbing system with both hot and cold water. I have laid out your soap and towels. Can you be ready for dinner in an hour?"

"Yes, ma'am. Thank you."

"You don't have to 'ma'am' me. I'm just plain Wilda."

Wilda disappeared with a lope, and Dorrie decided she would get along well with "just plain Wilda." Furthermore, the man of the house would have to be a terrible ogre to run her away from this paradise.

For the next hour, Dorrie was left to the mercies of her awe. She had never dreamed that anything so grand could be tucked away in this remote area. The governor couldn't lay claims to a more elaborate outlay.

Changes. Gabriel had warned her about them. She had been pitched back and forth from good to bad and bad to good with such celerity that she suffered emotional dizziness! The jail, so unspeakably hellish, made this place look like a veritable heaven. But what must the master of this grandeur be like, and why was he so hard to please? A ball of apprehension formed in Dorrie's chest at the thought of meeting such a monarch.

She slipped into a clean dress, her nicest, and brushed her hair, pulling it into a cool and becoming upsweep. Nellie believed that one must always put one's best foot forward when making new acquaintances. Dorrie wanted to look like an artist, a virtuoso who could paint a deserving portrait.

The dining room smelled of spices, and Dorrie's stomach rumbled. A lace-covered table deferred to the giant silver candelabrum in the center. Everything was state of the art. Dinner was a bountiful meal with joints of venison and beef, finished off with a light and delicious sponge cake, evidence of Wilda's busy day.

Unfortunately, the meal was disappointing for Dorrie. The master of the house did not show. She had hoped to meet him, to study his features in preparation for the canvas and brush.

Wilda made neither explanation nor excuse for Mr. Bronsworth's absence. She served Dorrie and Driver with the same savoir-faire she would have spent on a king. Dorrie ate and returned to her quarters with the uncanny sensation that although she had not seen him, Mr. Bronsworth had seen her from some hidden vantage.

Nor did she see Thaddeus Bronsworth on the following day. He seemed in no hurry to begin the picture sitting, and Dorrie, coddled by Wilda, luxuriated in the idle time for sketching, reading, and walking about the spacious yard where those who guarded her were virtually invisible.

## Chapter 20

# The Search

Time and an empty mailbox convinced Nellie that Dorrie had not reached her planned destination. Some tragedy had befallen her daughter. “Had she gotten there safely, we would have heard from her by now,” she told William. “I know the nature of my daughter. She is a responsible girl, and she would have written.”

Billy cried, unashamed of his tears, and Gabriel was not able to comfort him. “She said she’d write to me and to Dad and a three-times-as-long letter to Mom,” he sobbed. “I knew she hadn’t ought to go!”

Finally, Nellie’s heart-sore wrestlings took her to Martha Harris’s door. She needed someone to talk to, and even a husband sometimes did not understand a mother’s anxiety. Though past eighty, William’s mother still had a penchant for imparting her native wisdom to her loved ones in stormy times. She was their anchor.

Before Nellie put her hand on the screen, Martha’s voice found her. “Come on in, Nellie.” It was as if the elderly woman had expected her visit.

Nellie saw the portrait that Dorrie had painted—saw how Dorrie had assimilated Martha's exquisite features and delicately chiseled face, transferring the miracle to canvas—and her eyes filled with tears at the sight of it. "It is my daughter's grandest work, a true masterpiece," she whispered.

"You have come to talk about Dorrie." Martha's path to the heart of a matter took no detours.

"Yes. I haven't heard a word from her."

"And you are afraid that she won't return?"

"I'm—afraid that something—bad—has happened to her."

"She's likely busy with her new family, Nellie."

Nellie dropped into a pool of contemplation. Here she sat before an indefatigable woman who had committed a husband, a child, and a grandchild to the grave, her soul to God, and each of her living children to their chosen ambitions. Martha Harris knew how to let go. Nellie only knew how to hold on. She felt small and convicted.

Martha gave her daughter-in-law space, neither rushing nor prodding her. The younger woman needed ample leisure to gird up her dignity, to scotch her fears. So Martha waited.

"I guess I don't want to lend my daughter to another family. And that's uncharitable, isn't it?"

"Love covers a *multitude*, Nellie. Th' Bible says so. Dorrie can love you an' still love others. You an' Dorrie made a bow knot that life can never untie."

"But she is *my* daughter."

"If'n she belongs to you, she'll be back. If'n she doesn't return, she was never yours to start with. A thing held by force isn't yours. Dorrie is bumpin' on twenty-one. She has a right to her own choices. Holdin' a pretty butterfly too tightsome will only crush its wings so's it can't fly anymore."

The hands that Nellie placed over her eyes trembled and quivered against her face. "Yes, Mama Harris, that is so. I just needed to hear you say it. Thank you."

"Turn everything into God's hands, and leave it with Him."

"I will try to do that."

However, Nellie's resolve to leave her worries with God didn't last.

"Will we never know?" she badgered William. "There is no torment worse than the unknown. Even knowing that Dorrie was—killed—would be easier than this uncertainty."

Divested of a family himself, Gabriel Holt could hardly bear to witness the grief of the Harrises. He watched Nellie grow thinner, her face abused with apprehension. William was somber, too, finally admitting that something must have happened to Dorrie.

"I will make a trip to Seminole and see if she ever arrived there," offered Gabriel. "In a town so small, someone will know if she was there even for a few hours."

Nellie's gratitude showed in her tired eyes. "We will finance this trip, Gabriel."

"No, Mrs. Harris, it is something I want to do on my own. The crops are laid by, and I have nothing better for which to spend my money. Your Dorrie meant a lot to me, too." He fixed his eyes on the ceiling. "I—I think that I have been in love with your daughter for three years."

"Gabriel! I didn't know."

"And I *must* believe, Mrs. Harris, that Dorrie is alive somewhere. My heart will not discharge me to believe anything else. God has a way of protecting His children even in enemy territory."

"Pray that I may believe it, too, Gabriel. As Grandmother Harris says, 'A mother can't see the forest for the trees.' That was her way of saying that the answers to our prayers may be very near, but we cannot see them because we are seeking so hard."

Gabriel squandered no time in setting out, impatient to get on with his mission. But what if he didn't find her? A shaft of dread lanced him as he boarded the train. A sting hit his eyelids. *Please, God, lead me to her.*

The trip lagged interminably to love-bitten Gabriel. He ate without tasting, looked without seeing. A wagon road ran parallel to the railway where riders of horses reined up to await the train's passing. At any other time, this would have commanded Gabriel's interest. Under other circumstances, he would have noticed the straggle of derelict buildings, a-tilt in several directions at once. He would have enjoyed seeing the prairie dog villages that covered acres of the flats with small, taupe creatures sitting erect on their mounds. Now nothing mattered. If something dreadful had happened to the girl he adored, his life would have no meaning.

At Seminole he wasted no time, left no stones unturned in his inquiry. He talked to Mrs. Hogue, where Dorrie had slept, and interviewed Mr. York, where Dorrie had eaten. His relief was immense when he learned that she had accomplished this much of her journey safely and was well when she left, but he still couldn't relax. He had to find her.

Next, he interrogated the closed-mouth driver who transported Dorrie to Tulia on the supply wagon, learning little. He traced Dorrie's path to Mr. Trotter's hotel and spoke with the politician Trotter, who recommended that he talk with his son, Knight. Knight had gone to a party, and Gabriel was obliged to wait another day for the meeting.

The room he rented was well furnished, but it appeared that some cowboy had forgotten to remove his boots before he reposed. The sheets were dirtier than the floor. However, none of life's inconveniences fazed Gabriel. The only important thing was finding that Dorrie was alive.

The conference with Knight perturbed Gabe. Knight was impudent and slanderous. He misrepresented the truth to the point of outright lying. "Oh, yes," he said, cocking his handsome head to one side, "I knew Dorrie Harris, all right. I knew her well; a bit too well, I'm afraid. She and I were engaged to be married."

Gabriel drew in his breath. Knight noticed, purposely adding to Gabriel's discomfort. "She was a little vamp, that one. She went wild when she got to West Texas. The mollycoddled kind usually do. I thought she was being true to me, but was I fooled! She was slipping out with a dozen others.

"Oh, she pretended to be Miss Goody-Two-Shoes, but she was rotten down to the soles of her wandering feet!"

Gabriel cleared his throat, demanding attention with a short cough. "I think, sir, that we are not talking about the same young lady."

"Green eyes and copper hair?" Knight gave a snort of mocking laughter. "Yes, Mr. Holt, I'm afraid we are discussing the same subject matter. In fact, she mentioned your name to me. She said you were a student in her art class and that she once thought she could love you, but now it was out of sight and out of mind, and she would have her fling."

The words bit hard. Still, Gabriel must locate Dorrie for Nellie's sake. If he could talk Dorrie into going home, save her from her degradation, or even convince her to write a letter . . .

"Where—where is she now?"

"You don't want to know."

"I do want to know."

"She was caught at her little game and was sent to jail. She is paying her dues in Silverton behind the courthouse."

"I don't believe you."

"So you're calling me a liar?" Knight clenched his fists.

"*My* Dorrie was a Christian."

"My Dorrie!" Knight howled. "Those words crossed my tongue once, but I wouldn't have her now if she were made of gold," he said. "I will invite you to talk to Mr. Bill Briggs, the constable of Silverton, Mr. Holt. He will tell you how she came to his town as an impostor and caused nothing but havoc. And when you find Miss Harris, please be kind enough not to mention me. Her ears aren't fit to hear my name again—ever."

Gabriel's mind reeled and rebelled. He would not ask—yea, he would not allow—Knight to take him to Silverton. The man's heart was as black as pitch; he possessed a deformed soul given to evil humor. Waves of hot anger crashed in upon Gabriel. A thousand thronging sensations came and went. Incredulity. Dread. Fear. Confusion.

He walked the twenty miles to Silverton and went directly to the jail house, keeping his eyes averted from the dark, barred windows. One glance at the dreadful place made him ashamed that he had even come, that he had entertained a thought that he would find a virtuous girl like Dorrie here.

"Looking for someone?" the jailer asked, causing Gabriel to jump.

"Is—is there anyone in this place?"

"Not a soul," answered the jailer. "I'm required to stay in case the constable brings someone in, though."

"There hasn't been anyone here in a while, huh?"

"It's been several days now. You won't believe this, mister, but the last person I guarded was a woman."

"A woman?" Swallowing made a commotion in Gabe's neck.

"Yup. A young one at that. Green eyes and goldish hair. Lawsy, I had a time getting her to eat anything. She was a city slicker that didn't cotton to our cabbage stew."

"What was her reason for being here?"

"Some say one thing and some another. The town is split down the middle over it. Some declare she was picked up for bootlegging. They're on the constable's side. Other avow she was framed and wasn't guilty at all. That group includes the parson and his wife. The county sheriff was for fining her and letting her go."

"What was her name?"

"Last name of Harris. Did you know her?"

"I—I once knew a Miss Harris, but—"

"She was a fetching little thing when they first

brought her in. Twentyish. But it didn't take her long to break down. Bad food, poor sanitation. A woman's constitution is weaker than a man's, I allow. They shouldn't keep a woman in a place like this."

"Where is she now?"

"That very question has this town in an uproar. She got sick, and they sent her off to a hospital, but—" he spat toward his shoes, "but they waited too long to give her medical help. That's why the town is yapping. She never made it back."

The thought of Dorrie's death fell upon Gabriel, overwhelming him.

"You weren't her kin, were you?" asked the jailer.

"No. But I—I loved her. I came in behalf of her mother, who was worried—"

"Well, sir, we found a packet of letters backed to a Mr. William Harris, and we debated about what to do with them. The postage stamps had been torn off, and the city wasn't willing to pay for their delivery."

"I will take them to Mr. Harris."

Dreadful hours followed, full of questions. The road home stretched endlessly as the train chugged its way eastward. How could Gabriel face Nellie and tell her that her daughter was dead, her youth and sweetness tragically lost in a hideous mix-up on the high plains of Texas? They would never know where she was buried, could never visit her grave with bouquets of flowers.

They would suffer through all the stages of grief, individually, he and the Harris family: disbelief, denial, anger, and—at length—acceptance. The last stage, he told himself, was a long way off, for with the death of Dorrie Harris, Gabriel Holt's hopes and dreams died, too.

Chapter 21

# The Meeting

September's halcyon days waved a good-bye to summer. Dorrie had begun to wonder if there was even such a man as Thaddeus Bronsworth or if, perchance, the doctor had simply arranged this getaway for her mental and physical restoration. Then she decided that the driver who brought her to Bronsworth Estates was really Thaddeus Bronsworth.

A week passed with no mention of her starting to work. She appreciated the tranquillity of the sublime setting where people were kind and the food delectable, but she needed to be earning money for her fine.

She was anxious that her record be cleansed, after which she would return to her *real* home, where she would find love and warmth. For the rest of her life, she would be the world's best daughter.

When the feeling that she was accomplishing nothing threatened to overpower her, Dorrie spoke to Wilda. "I understand that I am being employed to paint a portrait of Mr. Bronsworth," she said. "When will Mr. Bronsworth be home so that I may begin?"

"Oh, he has been home all the while," replied Wilda. "He is in no hurry to begin." Her reaction confirmed Dorrie's suspicion that Driver was the man she would be working with.

"But I need to be earning money."

"You are earning money. Your employment began the first day you arrived. You will be paid well."

"It isn't fair that I should draw a wage when I am doing nothing at all," protested Dorrie. "Is there an old picture of Mr. Bronsworth that I may study in preparation for the painting?"

"Mr. Bronsworth has never had a portrait made of himself. None that was ever completed, anyway," Wilda said.

"I'm eager to begin so that I may get back to my home."

"I will tell him."

Quite by accident, Dorrie met the master of the house. She had walked to the barn and found the door standing ajar. The barn, a huge affair with a wide lane through the center, had stalls on either side. A horse nickered, sending Dorrie in search of it.

Her exploration took her to the tack room. She peered inside just as Thaddeus Bronsworth raised his head from the repairing of a saddle. Consternation ran through her, but she allowed none of the shock to reach the surface and undermine her composure. Mr. Bronsworth's face with its lipless mouth was massively scarred. One of his eyes had an alarming inability to focus. No wonder no one wanted to paint his picture!

Dorrie's well-trained demeanor functioned automatically. She flashed him a warm, friendly smile, "Pardon me for interrupting your work, sir. It looks as though you are doing a classic job."

He tried to return her smile, but the result was a miserable grimace. "I am Thaddeus Bronsworth, and you must be my artist," he said, a note of apology riding low in his throat.

"Yes, sir, and I am hoping to begin our project right away."

"Are you comfortable in your room? Have you everything you need?"

"Oh, yes, sir! You run a most efficient household."

"Do you like horses?"

"Very much, sir. My daddy, William, taught me to ride before my feet reached the stirrups. But I haven't ridden in—in a long time."

"Would you like to ride?"

Dorrie's face lighted with gladness. "Oh, yes! That is, if you don't mind."

"I'll saddle Lady Hatbox for you," he said, pulling a heavy leather saddle from the rack. "She's as gentle as a kitten and twice as worthless." He led the way to one of the paddocks. "She is a bit overfed and more than a little spoiled, like everything else on this ranch." He made a noise that sounded like a laugh but didn't look like one.

Leading out a lovely chestnut mare, he asked, "Would you mind if I ride along with you? I could show you over the property."

"The constable would be most happy," she bantered. "I am a wicked criminal, you know, and he is anticipating my escape."

"I might help you escape," he chuckled.

The trail they followed skirted the Canadian River, sometimes dropping into the shallow arroyos where sudden washes had gouged the land. Old trees, some covered with lichen, some split by lightning, wore a crown of leaves flowing green and silver in the breeze. The wind bathed her face, and Dorrie felt exhilaration. If only she could ride forever and not have to worry about constables or jails or fines!

By the time they returned to the barn, the sun hung low in the west, causing the leaves on the cottonwoods to shimmer like new quarters. Dorrie's mind was invigorated, her spirit refreshed. "Thank you for a lovely ride, Mr. Bronsworth," she said. Her eyes twinkled. "And I didn't even try to break and run, did I?"

"We'll ride again tomorrow if you wish, Miss Harris."

"Only after I've begun my work, Mr. Bronsworth. All play and no work makes Dorrie a shiftless girl. I didn't come here to loaf and collect wages for my laziness."

That evening Mr. Bronsworth joined them for dinner. Dorrie brought her sense of humor to the forefront, reiterating funny incidents from her childhood to make the meal a relaxed and enjoyable occasion. Why would anyone find it difficult to get along with these people?

Mr. Bronsworth chose the library as the location for the portrait's setting. A glass-fronted bookcase gobbled up one entire wall, and Dorrie teased that he had more books than her school library. It wasn't far from the truth. His good eye followed her head as she turned it to look at his anthology. "Do you like to read?" he asked.

"It is my favorite pastime."

"You are free to borrow anything from my library anytime you wish."

"Work first," she reminded. "If I start reading those wonderful analects, I'll not get a thing done."

She brought out her paints, set up her easel, and unrolled the canvas. "Have you a time frame, Mr. Bronsworth, for our work? Shall we allow, say, two hours at a stretch for the portrait? More than that might tire both of us. I pride myself in working rather swiftly. We will be finished before you know it." In her mind she struggled: How could she paint such a face?

Thaddeus Bronsworth said nothing. He sat tensely and quietly while she put the first strokes on the white backdrop. Dorrie feared that he might bolt any minute. He was a different man here than he had been yesterday as they rode across his land or tonight at the dinner table. She felt such sympathy for his stress that she cut the setting short, reckoning she could gradually ease into longer periods of composition.

However, the next session was no better, only worse. She suggested that they rest the following afternoon, and on that day they rode again, stopping in the speckled shade of a mesquite tree for Mr. Bronsworth to point out an orange ocotillo flower crouching against the ground. It was Dorrie's first glimpse of the man's soul, a man so destitute of beauty yet a man who could admire the most delicate of God's creations.

When she resumed the painting again, the nervousness returned. On the fourth day, he could sit no longer. He hurled himself from the high-backed chair where he posed. "I can't go through with it," he said. "I'm sorry."

So this is where the previous artists had met their Waterloo. She wouldn't let it happen to her. "Mr. Bronsworth," she said firmly, "I have yet to abandon a project that I start, and I don't intend to do so now. I am doing quite well so far, and we will see this portrait through to completion. Then, if you don't like my work, you can destroy it at your leisure. Please be seated."

Mr. Bronsworth sat down, his whole body trembling with the effort. "I—surely you understand—"

"Let me ask you a question, Mr. Bronsworth. How many times have you aborted a photographic endeavor?"

"More times than I can count."

"For some reason unknown to me, you have employed an artist to make a portrait of yourself. I have been chosen to do the work. I am not a quitter, and I would ask that you show the same steadfast quality, please. If you find that you cannot do it, I will not take *one dime* of your money. I—" her voice shook, "I would rather sit my fine out in that miserable jail house with the mice than take money for work I did not do!"

## Chapter 22

# The Letters

Spurred by confusion and unrest, Nellie took the packet of letters that Dorrie had written in Tule Canyon and headed for Brazos Point to Martha Harris's house. When distress knocked at her door, she wanted her mother-in-law beside her to meet the collector. Martha had a godly wisdom, a way of putting things in perspective. What would the family do without her, their foundation stone? *I hope she lives to be a hundred,* Nellie thought.

"Sit yerself down a spell, Nellie," Martha said as Nellie came through the front door. "Weather's nice, isn't it? But you didn't come to talk about th' weather. Somethin's matterin' your heart. An' it's Dorrie. I told you, she'll be returnin' a much wiser an' better lassie. She'll come back appreciatin' things she took fer granted afore. She'll—"

After a speechless moment, Nellie broke the news. "Dorrie isn't coming back, Mama Harris. Our Dorrie is—is dead."

"Surely you've mistaked it, Nellie," argued the old

woman as she pushed herself forward in the horsehair chair. "I didn't get a death warnin' from God, an' I've always got 'em before. Oh, yes, I knew Dorris was goin' through some tryin' times, 'cause I felt it here," she put her hand on her heart, "but—but are you positive about her bein' dead?"

"Yes, Mama Harris."

"How did you get th' word?"

"When we heard nothing from Dorrie, a friend of ours, Gabriel Holt, went to see if he could find her. His road dead-ended in a place called Silverton. Someone told him that she took sick and died."

"An' you never heard a word from her?"

"That's the fluke of it, Mama Harris. Gabriel brought back a whole pack of letters that Dorrie had written. They had never been mailed. Not a one of them. Someone had torn off the stamps. The envelopes are weathered, and on some of them the ink is hardly legible." She pulled the letters from her purse. "With these letters, it is hard to believe that she is really gone."

"What say th' letters?"

"They're typical Dorrie style. She told all about her trip, and she sent some sketches she drew. She found her paternal grandparents—"

"She did?"

"They run a general store in Tule Canyon. She writes that her grandmother was not in good health when she arrived, but with Dorrie's care she improved. She sent her love to Billy and William and said she missed us all. She was eager for a letter from us, but of course, we didn't know where to write since we did not receive her letters."

"Now, if that's not peculiar! But why don't you read

me one of th' letters?"

Nellie's fingers fluttered against the stationery. *Dear Mom,* she read. *Life is much different here, which makes me the more thankful for the way you taught me.*

"Yep, that's Dorrie all right," interspersed Martha. "Always thankful."

*My grandparents do not know our Jesus, but I am doing my best to introduce them to Him. Perhaps I was sent here for that purpose. Can you imagine me being a missionary?*

"Sure as the world I can, Dorrie," answered Martha.

*Grandmother Dorris (her name is Iantha) has terrible headaches. She is seldom able to cook or keep house, so I have taken over that responsibility. She has never stopped grieving over the death of my father.*

"Then Dorrie's father is dead," commented Martha. "An' she never knowed him."

*Grandmother has his picture buried in a box behind the barn, and periodically she uncovers it to look at it once more. I hope that I may paint a portrait of her son for her from the small one she has. I would like to see his picture, to know what he looks like, but I have not been here long enough to feel my freedom to ask. She seems very protective of it, but she will come to trust me eventually.*

"Humph. Seems to me a grandma would offer to show a girl her own papa's picture."

*You would be proud of my dumplings, Mom. They taste almost as good as yours. And Grandfather Dorris loves my bread pudding.*

*I am running short of funds for reasons I'd rather*

*not discuss at this time, but Grandfather has promised that I might put in a few hours a week at the store.*

"She took a-plenty, didn't she?" muttered Martha, but Nellie kept reading.

*The wage will not be good, but I will have change for stamps and personal supplies.*

*There is a young man who is calling on me (his name is Knight). He seems nice, but I must know God's will in the matter of a lifetime commitment. I want a solid marriage such as you and Daddy have. Please make this a matter of prayer.*

*Give Daddy and Billy and Grandmother Harris a big hug for me. Love, Dorrie.*

Nellie folded the letter. "When I read these letters, she doesn't seem dead," she said, burying her face in her hands. "I am so confused!"

"Where did your friend find the letters?" Martha asked.

Nellie hesitated. Should she burden Martha with the knowledge?

"From—uh—the jailer."

"The *jailer*?"

"I know, Mama Harris. Nothing makes sense. Gabriel didn't see or talk to the grandparents at all. The jailer said that a Susan Harris had been picked up on a charge of selling liquor and that she had no known relatives—"

"Then it wasn't our Dorrie. There might be several Susan Harrises."

"Except the jailer described her, and she had these letters in her handbag."

"Someone could've been impersonating her; they

might have stolen her handbag."

"Gabriel talked with the young man she mentioned, Knight. She had told him about me and you. And William and Billy."

"And she died in the jail?"

"No, they sent her to a hospital somewhere, and—and she never returned."

"There's too many open gaps in th' story, Nellie. B'fore you draw up any tight-minded conclusions, you need to know more than hearsay."

"We sent a telegram to Mr. and Mrs. Dorris at Tule Canyon and asked that they return their answer collect. But we haven't heard from them."

"I ain't b'lievin' Dorrie is dead until God lets me know. Which He gen'rally does. And He hasn't."

## CHAPTER 23

# The Unburdening

Dorrie wasn't sure what Mr. Bronsworth's decision would be in regard to her completing his portrait. Uncertainties and fears assailed her. She had opened her mouth and told him she would refuse any payment unless he let her complete the work. Her pride would not let her recant.

She couldn't blame the man for not wanting his distorted face put on canvas, yet there was a strength of character in that face that surpassed the ugliness. He was one of the kindest men she had ever met. She must capture this inner softness with her brush and bring it into view. She had done it with Grandmother Harris, and she could do it again. But would Mr. Bronsworth endure until she finished?

According to the doctor, her fine must be paid in sixty days. Time was running out; every day that Mr. Bronsworth delayed brought her closer to the deadline. If her subject decided to disband the whole idea, where would she get the money to pay her way out of this quagmire? If payment was not forthcoming, she would go back to that horrible cell. Her heart plummeted at the thought.

Needing the balm of the outdoors, she edged away from the house. With her arms folded across the fence post that was so new she could smell the resin, she looked toward the east. Would she ever get back home? Billy would be back in school now. Nellie would be quilting for winter. Gabriel would be harvesting pumpkins and turnips and cotton. . . . She dropped her head, and warm tears bathed her arms.

"You are not trying an elusive escape, are you?" Mr. Bronsworth's voice held laughter. The creak of the windmill had drowned out his footfalls, and she had not heard his approach. As if snapping from a paralysis, her tear-streaked face lifted.

"Oh, I am sorry," he apologized with such genuine regret that Dorrie felt a pang of pity for him. He laid a hand on her shoulder very gently. "Miss Harris, is there anything I can do to—to take away your pain and make you feel better?"

"You are a Christian, aren't you, Mr. Bronsworth?"

"Yes, I am. I was brought to Calvary by my captain when I was in the Navy. We became close friends; he was much like a father to me and I a son to him. Then came the—the explosion on the ship and the—the terrible fire. I pulled my captain from the flames. I survived, but he lived only a few days. But there, that's all behind and heaven is ahead, and I must not burden you with any of it."

"I would like to hear all of your story."

"Perhaps some day, Miss Harris, but not now. I have

never told it to anyone."

"Since you are a Christian, will you pray for me? It seems that my prayers are not getting through to God."

"I have prayed for you every day since you arrived, and I will continue to do so. I will be glad to take any burden that you may have to the throne of God, and I will be glad to share your sorrow. I have no contact with the outside world for obvious reasons. I cannot bear to frighten little children with my grotesque disfigurement. But I do have contact with a world more real than the one we stand on."

The human compassion, offered so freely, left Dorrie nonplused. The misery girdled in her soul pushed against its restraining staves, breaking them. "Oh, sir," she cried brokenly. "I am guilty of no crime. I did nothing to warrant a prison sentence. There was a mistake somewhere—!"

"Would you like to start at the beginning and tell me what happened, Miss Harris?"

"Yes. I had gone to Tule Canyon in search of my roots. You see, I was adopted by the Harris family when I was seven years old. My real name is Susan Dorris. My mother died, and I never knew my father. Some unrest propelled me to the venture, a calling for knowledge such as Mother Eve must have experienced in the garden and passed on to all womankind. It was a quest of my own choosing without God's blessings."

"Was your adoptive family kind to you, Susan?"

"Oh, very, sir! They gave me the best they could offer: a comfortable home, a good education, a godly example, and unconditional love. I became an art teacher in a local school. I enjoyed my job and loved my students. I was foolish to gamble on a youthful fantasy. I was the loser. It all seems so long ago and in another world—"

Mr. Bronsworth was a good listener; he didn't interrupt or break in with lame advice.

"But what is done is done. Anyway, in a place called Seminole, I learned that my father had died. He had deserted my mother before I was born. He had a police record and was quite irresponsible. Through his records, I found my grandparents. They lived in the canyon near Silverton. I discovered an overworked grandfather and a sick grandmother. But worse yet, they were not Christians. I felt it my obligation to stay and introduce them to Jesus. It's so—so heartbreaking to think that none of my birth family are saved and that—that my father went to meet God unprepared."

Mr. Bronsworth, touched by Dorrie's story, wiped away tears of his own.

Dorrie gave a crooked smile. "Grandmother Harris says that looking back is an old person's ploy. I must be getting old."

"You haven't told me about your 'crime.'"

"I'm getting there. I was living with my grandparents and working part-time in their grocery store. I was making a delivery for my grandfather, Slocum Dorris, when the constable arrested me. I had taken a jar of pickling vinegar to one of our customers, and—and the officer said it was whiskey."

"Your grandfather didn't straighten up the matter with the constable?"

"When I was put in jail, it brought such shame to the Dorris name that they disowned me. Everyone abandoned me, even the young man who professed to love me. My heart and mind and body were driven close to their ultimate limits."

Mr. Bronsworth said nothing.

"The doctor at the hospital said that I would have died in jail had not the county sent me to a good medical facility." Here she stopped and placed her hand on his arm. "And oh, sir, I am so grateful that you had the hospital built, or I would not be alive today!"

The recognition of his good deed embarrassed Mr. Bronsworth, so Dorrie hurried on. "I—I can't bear the thoughts of going back to jail when I know that I didn't do anything to deserve the punishment. I—I could have paid my fine and been released before now if—if my money hadn't been—" She cut the disclosure short, sorry that she had let it slip.

"Sometimes, Susan," Mr. Bronsworth said slowly, "God is nearest when He seems the farthest away. Remember the verse that says, 'Lo, I am with you alway'? He promised never to leave us or forsake us. And this one: 'All things work together for good to them that love God, to them who are the called according to His purpose.' Though you may not understand this portion of your life today, you will understand it in a better tomorrow. Please be assured that He is holding your hand at this moment."

*Gabe had made that same statement.*

"Remember Joseph? He was wrongfully accused and unjustly thrown in prison. Does that sound familiar?"

Dorrie nodded.

"Yet God had a plan, and Joseph kept trust in his trustworthy God." Mr. Bronsworth gave the smiling grimace. "Several of God's favorite people spent time in jail: Joseph, Jeremiah, John the Baptist, Peter, Paul. . . . You must be special to Him."

"Thank you, Mr. Bronsworth, for listening. You have helped me."

That afternoon, Mr. Bronsworth did not show up for his setting. He left Dorrie a note in the library. An emergency had arisen, it said, and he would be away for a few hours. He had decided to permit her to complete his portrait. He welcomed her to browse through his books in his absence.

A brace of wild geese chose that evening to honk their way south, so high in the sky that they looked like cobwebs drifting in the wind. Dorrie's mind flew with them, refusing to slow. She was in a frantic race with time. Mr. Bronsworth didn't seem to realize that time squeezed her, that the picture must be completed by the middle of October or the constable would send his posse for her. The posing had taken on a maddening hit-and-miss consistency, and in spite of all Mr. Bronsworth said, she still feared that he would not follow through. If he reneged, she would spend the cold, dark days of winter behind bars.

Mr. Bronsworth had refused to view the portrait. "How is it coming, Miss Harris?" he would inquire occasionally.

"Very well, Mr. Bronsworth. I think you will like it. But I really must work faster. Time is running out."

What Dorrie did not know is that Thaddeus Bronsworth had gone to town for the first time in many years. Moved by her story, he had taken himself there in her behalf to obtain her release. He endured the stares, turned a deaf ear to the gasps of women and a blind eye to the rude fingers of pointing children to pay her fine so that she might go free.

He believed every word of her story. He believed her innocent.

Thaddeus reached up and ran his hand across the scars. *I cannot tell her what she means to me, yet I cannot let her go*, he told himself. Keeping her at work on the portrait was buying time, but how he dreaded having to behold the finished work!

CHAPTER 24

# Completed Project

The closer the strokes of Dorrie's brush brought the portrait to completion, the more apprehensive Mr. Bronsworth became. Dorrie understood why all previous artists had given up. She would be tempted to do the same if she didn't have so much at stake. It seemed cruel to make a human endure such agony of spirit. Why was he determined that his picture be made anyway?

Dorrie had ceased to think of Mr. Bronsworth's appearance as unpleasant. His kindness, his generosity of spirit, his inner integrity so eclipsed the physical manifestation that she seldom thought of the scars at all. He had, in fact, a stateliness that escaped mere eyesight but could rather be felt. It was impossible to determine his age, but here was a princely man who would live and die in his lonely world: friendless, companionless, and childless. Dorrie considered that a regrettable destiny.

*Gabriel Holt would like Mr. Bronsworth.* He would love the ranch, the clear air, the brilliance of the stars at night, millions of them beyond counting. *Gabriel* . . . In a flashback, Dorrie heard his voice, felt the pressure of his hand on hers, saw the eyes that tried to convey a message to her. *I love you, Dorrie.* Suddenly, she wanted to proclaim it to the world: *Gabe! Gabe! Can you hear me? I love you, too!*

The days were noticeably shorter as September elbowed into October. Now Dorrie's goal was to get home before the holidays. She had to admit she rather dreaded leaving the ranch; Wilda and Mr. Bronsworth were spoiling her.

When a premature cold spell moved in, she and Thaddeus Bronsworth played checkers in front of the fireplace. Mr. Bronsworth was good at the game—much better than Billy—but she had played enough to give him a healthy challenge. He often forgot himself and shook with a full, hearty laugh when she made a cunning capture.

One evening after they had especially enjoyed each other's companionship, Dorrie reminded Mr. Bronsworth that she would be able to wrap up her work by week's end. That would give her a grace period of three days to be freed from her status as a criminal. She could now finish the picture, she said, with or without her subject's cooperation.

To Dorrie's disappointment, Mr. Bronsworth did not appear the next day for their appointment. She painted alone in the library, finding it a large and empty place. Until today, she had considered it a special room; now she knew that it was he who made the room special. Without him, it was a lonely, walled space of boards and plaster. Nor did Mr. Bronsworth show up for any of the meals that day. Wilda said that he had left before daylight, and she did not know where he had gone or why.

Dorrie put the finishing touches on the picture and then backed away to survey the canvas in its entirety. She had accomplished what she set out to do and was immensely satisfied. This one work of art unsheathed the expertise of her talent. Although the substantial scars were in bold evidence, there was an underlying aura that took dominance over them. It bespoke an inner virtue, commanding the greater of one's attention, subtly minimizing the physical harshness of the imperfect face. This masterpiece proved to the world that Thaddeus Bronsworth was an exceptional man, worthy of the love of a woman, a child, and creation at large.

It was done. Dorrie laid her head on Mr. Bronsworth's oaken desk and cried. She cried from sheer relief and for pure joy and for other reasons that didn't make sense.

When Mr. Bronsworth returned, Dorrie insisted that he see the picture to be sure it pleased him. He was sick all night before the viewing; he came to breakfast nauseous and weak. As the time came to go to the library for the unveiling, he steadied himself by gripping the door frame before he entered. "I'll just pay you and look later when I am alone," he told Dorrie.

"No, Mr. Bronsworth." Dorrie was adamant. "I must know before I leave if my work is acceptable."

"It will be acceptable, Susan."

"Please, Mr. Bronsworth," she said, resorting to entreaty. "Remember that I have put many hours of my life into this."

His palms were damp with perspiration. "May I sit?"

"Surely."

She turned the picture toward him, stepping aside so

that he could get the full impact of his impression.

His hands clung to the sides of the chair, and he stared for long, silent moments. *Was he pleased?* Finally, his head went down, and tears dripped onto his shirt.

Dorrie ran to him, putting her arms about his broad shoulders. She had failed! "You don't like it, Mr. Bronsworth?"

"It's just that—that—" His words snagged on some jagged emotion. "I haven't looked in a mirror since the accident. I—I look so much better than I remember. Susan, you have made my face look like a human. Are you sure this—this is me?"

"This is exactly the way you look to me, Mr. Bronsworth, and I have very good vision. You have a special handsomeness that few people ever attain. Some people are beautiful on the outside, but you are beautiful inside, which is the greatest gift of all. And it shows, you see."

Looking at the portrait, he blurted, "I—I almost feel that I could be loved by—by someone if they could see me as you do—"

"Of course!" Had she ever felt more fulfillment? She wanted to dance around the room like a delighted child. "You will remember, sir, that Christ had scars. His visage was marred more than any man's—more than yours. And many of us love Him the more for His scars. Scars are sacred. They speak of bravery and heroism."

"By painting the picture, you—you have changed my life, Susan. You see, I—" He started to reveal more and then broke off abruptly. "I will miss you, but you must return to the people, the adoptive family, who have invested so much into your life. You are a daughter of whom they can be proud and an artist that I can recommend to anyone. I will never forget you," he lowered his voice as well as his eyes, "and I hope that you will never forget me."

"Oh, sir, I never could forget you! I came on a quest to find my natural family, but I have found something better: another member of my spiritual family. For if I have learned any lesson at all from my bitter experience, it is that one's roots count for little. God's grafting is the important thing, so that we may bear fruit for Him."

"You are a wise young lady, Susan. May God go with you. I will say good-bye. Driver has your check. He will take you back to the doctor in Amarillo, who will be responsible for your release papers."

In a moment of intense gratitude, Dorrie flung her arms about her benefactor and wept at the parting. He had saved her name, her honor, and her life.

## Chapter 25

# Home

When Dorrie reached her room to prepare for her departure, an elegant green dress, a corded bengaline tinted to the shade of her eyes, lay on her bed. The skirt's shirring fell over a narrow frill at the bottom, and roses made of fabric added to its charm. Dorrie had never seen a dress so lovely. A card that accompanied it read: *For your 21st birthday, whenever it was. T. B.* Dorrie tried to swallow over the lump precipitated by Mr. Bronsworth's thoughtfulness. Knowing that she likely would not see him again before she left, she wrote him a simple note expressing her delight with the gift. Then she took one last look at the ranch, a place that had been a haven to her, and climbed into the car.

Driver took her to town and, in parting, placed a long, white envelope in her hand. It was her wages, a check for forty dollars, the exact amount she needed.

The doctor was surprised to see her. "I have come to pay my fine," she told him.

He looked puzzled. "Your fine?"

"The forty dollars."

"Oh, that has already been taken care of, Miss Harris," the doctor said.

"The charges were dropped?"

"The fine was paid last month by—by a friend of yours. You are free to go. Your friend also insisted that your record be completely cleared, and that has been done."

*It is the gratuity of Mr. Bronsworth,* she told herself.

With forty dollars in her hand, she had funds for travel, for food, and enough left to last until she could find another teaching job. There was no need to write home; she'd be there by the time a letter arrived. She would surprise them!

Excitement boiled in her blood. Had it only been five months since she'd seen them? It seemed more like a decade.

The train from Amarillo took her east into Oklahoma Station then south along the Chisholm stage trail. She expected some metamorphosis beyond the borders of her home state—snow-capped mountains or gold mines or towering rock formations—but there was nothing except a sameness of scenery. The conversion, she decided, was all within herself. Nothing in the caves and valleys and meadows of her heart would ever be the same. *Changes? Yes, Gabriel, there were changes. But when I get home, I hope there will be even more changes. . . .*

Dorrie slept a great deal of the way back. The abuse of her sensitive nature had brought exhaustion of mind and spirit. Thoughts of Thaddeus Bronsworth were drowned in her anticipation of rejoining William, Nellie, and Billy. She hoped that Grandmother Harris was well and that her unexplained absence had not occasioned undue grief for the elderly woman who bore the lion's share of the burdens of the entire Harris family.

Adorned in her new green outfit, she alit from the train at the Cleburne depot and looked about. She would need to hire a carriage for herself and her luggage.

Some might call it coincidence, but Dorrie declared forever after that it was the plan of God. Returning from the gin where he had taken his cotton to be baled, Gabriel Holt passed the train station just as Dorrie stepped from the platform. He saw her with her portmanteau at her feet, scanning the street for a conveyance to take her home. She thought she'd never forget the first unbelieving look in his eyes, a look that was half fearful as though he saw a vision and to move or to speak would shatter it.

He reined in so abruptly that the cotton wagon almost overran the horses. "Miss Harris!" he hailed. "Is that you? Are my eyes deceiving me?" He jumped down and was beside her in a trice.

"Gabe!" She reached out her hands, and he took them. "Yes, I'm home."

"And looking so beautiful! Oh, Dorrie, we thought you were dead!"

"*We*?"

"Your family and myself. My mother died, and William and Nellie Harris adopted me."

"And now you are Gabriel Harris?"

"No, I kept my name—"

Their eyes met, and Dorrie saw that the love was still there, the same love that she had seen in the classroom that memorable afternoon, only stronger.

"Good! I'd rather change my name to Holt than for you to change yours to Harris."

"Oh, my dear! Oh, Dorrie, do you mean it?" Gabriel's arms went around her, and he kissed her full on the lips, oblivious to the stares of passersby who probably wondered at an overall-clad cotton farmer embracing the well-dressed passenger who had just disembarked from a Pullman coach. "This is the happiest day of my life!"

"Mine, too, even if it will mean more changes." Caught between weeping and laughing, Dorrie evinced overwhelming joy.

Gabriel remembered where they stood and what his gentlemanly duties were. "This cotton wagon isn't very comfortable, dear. The seat is hardly wide enough for two. You'll have to sit very near and cling to me. But I promise only to let you fall one direction; that's *for* me." He winked, a cute, boyish motion.

"The nearer the better, Gabriel."

Nellie flirted with a faint when Gabriel brought Dorrie through the door, holding her hand. "Mom Harris, here she is. I brought her back to you, but only for a short while. Finders keepers, you know. I'm claiming her. Whatever she has been through, she looks more gorgeous today than she did when she left, doesn't she?"

Dorrie embraced Nellie. "Mother! I'm glad to be back. My heart is back. I'm sorry you didn't get my letters. It's a long story."

"I got them."

"You did? But how—?"

Nellie looked from Dorrie to Gabriel, wondering what had transpired between the two and where to start with the explaining. "Gabriel brought them home from

Silverton when he went looking for you."

"You came there—looking for me, Gabriel?" Dorrie's eyes widened, and her pulse quickened. A warm cocoon of certainty enveloped her. Had she been in jail, Gabe would have rescued her.

"Yes," Gabe said, "and I met with an incompetent liar named Knight whose duplicity you escaped."

"Thanks to God and your prayers."

"Then I was told that you had been taken to a hospital and—and that you never returned."

"I didn't return."

"But—but we thought that meant you had died."

"I almost did, but God spared me. He let me live to paint a picture and to return to my family. And to you."

It was an evening of celebration. Gabriel took Dorrie to see Grandmother Harris. "She's one grandmother in a million," Gabriel said, "and we don't want her to suffer unnecessarily one moment. I want her around for our own children to enjoy."

Into the deep of the night, after the household had fallen asleep, Dorrie lay wide-eyed, lost in rumination. She had wasted five months in a quest to find grandparents, aunts, and cousins who disowned her, to learn that her father was dead, and to paint one portrait: the picture of Thaddeus Bronsworth. It had been a futile quest.

*Or had it?*

## Chapter 26

# Quest's End

Plans for a holiday wedding crystallized. Dorrie's heart beat like the wings of an eagle, taking her to soaring heights. She loved Gabe, and he loved her.

For precious hours they talked, never getting enough of each other's nearness, enjoying the simple wonder of just being together. She laid every detail of her quest before him, withholding nothing. From her palette of colorful adjectives, she chose the most dulcet to describe Bronsworth Estates and its owner.

"It is a place of utter tranquillity," she said. "There is peace such as cannot be found in life's busy commotion. It's—it's like a beautiful and remote island where one could go and forget the outside world."

"It sounds like the ideal spot for a honeymoon!" Gabriel remarked.

"Indeed, it would be. Oh, Gabriel, I wish we could go there! You would get on grandly with Mr. Bronsworth; you wouldn't even mind his scars. And I know you'd like Lady Hatbox."

"Lady Hatbox?"

"She's one of Mr. Bronsworth's mares. We could ride horses by the river and read books by the fireplace and enjoy Wilda's sweet yeast kuchen while it's still warm and—"

"It sounds lovely, but we could hardly go without an invitation, darling."

In the aftermath of the conversation, Dorrie's mind still harvested blessings from her weeks on the ranch. The memory of Thaddeus Bronsworth—the things he had said, the kindness he had shown—scratched at her serenity, but she managed, for the most part, to push it to the back burner. Then the letter came.

"There's mail for you, Dorrie," Billy announced, pitching the envelope on the table. "It is addressed to Susan Harris, in care of Mr. William Harris, Cleburne, Texas. It looks like a man's script."

Thaddeus Bronsworth. Noting the return address—and being possessed by a dull, unplaced pain—Dorrie took the letter to her room to read it in private. A check for one hundred dollars fell from the confines of the container.

*I cannot accept charity from the man*, Dorrie told herself. *He is not indebted to me, nor I to him. I was merely an employed artist who did my best. I will return Mr. Bronsworth's check promptly.*

They had shared a special and unique friendship. They had needed each other, and even now she found that she was glad to hear from him.

*Dear Susan:* he wrote,

*Thank you for the happiness you brought to my life with your brief stay on the ranch. I miss you dread-*

*fully, but I am a changed man and entirely undeserving of God's forgiveness and revelation.*

*I almost brought myself to speak with you before you left, but my courage failed. I told you about my friend and his unfortunate death after the explosion on the ship, but I did not tell you the rest of the story.*

*I knew your grandparents well; I have known them all my life. I played with Mary and Lottie when I was small. Your grandfather has been a bootlegger for as long as I can remember, but he has always managed to sidestep the law. You were his pawn; he sent you to deliver whiskey to a customer then hadn't the stuff of a man in him to take the punishment himself. Rather, he denied any relationship with you to save his own skin. You did not disgrace him; he disgraced you.*

*Likewise, your grandmother has been an alcoholic for many years. She was not unearthing the picture of her deceased son from behind the barn as she led you to believe but was digging up her bottle for a drink. Her excessive drinking brought on the hangover headaches. I have seen her do this time and again.*

*I was also acquainted with your mother, Mattie, but that was before the birth of any of her children. Through the smudging of time, I remember her as a lovely girl who married much too young and suffered abuse at the hands of an unscrupulous man, her first husband. I was not aware that she had died, and I offer you my sympathy. You bear her likeness to an astonishing degree.*

*The man who led me to salvation, my Navy captain, gave me his property, his wealth, and his name when he died. My name is really Charles Dorris.*

*Please accept the check, my daughter. Where this came from, there is plenty more. When I am gone to heaven to meet your dear mother and await your coming, all that I have will be yours. God has filled my cup. Please remain with your lovely adopted family and make a life for yourself there. They have made of you a better woman than I could ever have hoped to do.*

*The ranch is open to you, your friends, and your family at any time. It is your home. Please feel welcome!*

*Love, Daddy Charles*

There was a postscript:

*Who would think*
*That we would be blessed*
*To find each other*
*In an artist's quest?*

# About the Author

LaJoyce Martin, a minister's wife, has written for Word Aflame Publications for many years with numerous stories and books in print. She is in much demand for speaking at seminars, banquets, and camps. Her writings have touched people young and old alike all over the world.